'*Little Gods* is a remarkable read, for its authentic voice and its use of the appealing Olive as an immature, and therefore unreliable, narrator . . . A gem, and not to be missed.' ***Better Reading***

'A ripping, sprawling family saga featuring an eccentric cast with an abundance of big secrets.' **Stella Prize judges' comments**

'There is charm in the passing details of an Australian childhood recalled and in Olive there is a winning lead character.' ***Sydney Morning Herald***

'*Little Gods* is a slice of life from days gone by and I loved the authenticity of it. It's about family, the good and the bad, loyalty and protection within, even when we don't like the people we're related to. It's about understanding that the truth can hurt and won't necessarily set you free.' **Theresa Smith Writes**

'*Little Gods* might just crush your heart.' ***Newtown Review of Books***

'Jenny Ackland has brought a recognisable world to the page and her characters are realised with empathy and catch at the heart.' **Readings**

PRAISE FOR

The Secret Son

'Ackland has given a first novel that reshapes familiar historical material with originality and dash . . . and offers pleasing indications of the present and future health of Australian fiction.' ***The Australian***

A fascinating read . . . Ackland weaves in the story of James from Gallipoli onwards into the story of Cem, and brings them together to create a mystery that evolves over the book to keep you reading.' **The Book Muse**

'Jenny Ackland's debut novel cleverly guides us into that space of suspension of disbelief where truths in fiction question the very essence of truth.' **Readings**

'Jenny Ackland's *The Secret Son* is a remarkable and exhilarating debut. At once joyous and haunting, and a moving meditation on love, honour and belonging, it is a story about the strength of women and what it means to be a good man.' ***Australian Arts Review***

Jenny Ackland is a writer, educator and podcaster from Melbourne. Her previous novels are *The Secret Son* and *Little Gods*. *Hurdy Gurdy* is her third novel.

HURDY GURDY

JENNY ACKLAND

ALLEN&UNWIN
SYDNEY • MELBOURNE • AUCKLAND • LONDON

First published in 2024

CREATIVE VICTORIA

This project is supported by the Victorian Government through Creative Victoria.

Allen & Unwin
Cammeraygal Country
83 Alexander Street
Crows Nest NSW 2065
Australia
Phone: (61 2) 8425 0100
Email: info@allenandunwin.com
Web: www.allenandunwin.com

Allen & Unwin acknowledges the Traditional Owners of the Country on which we live and work. We pay our respects to all Aboriginal and Torres Strait Islander Elders, past and present.

NATIONAL LIBRARY OF AUSTRALIA
A catalogue record for this book is available from the National Library of Australia

ISBN 978 1 76106 979 6

Set in 12.2/19.2 pt Minion Pro by Bookhouse, Sydney
Printed and bound in Australia by the Opus Group

10 9 8 7 6 5 4 3 2 1

FSC www.fsc.org MIX Paper | Supporting responsible forestry FSC® C001695

The paper in this book is FSC® certified. FSC® promotes environmentally responsible, socially beneficial and economically viable management of the world's forests.

FOR LILY

I am a sad and ragged little guy who is very serious about everything he attempts—no matter how futile or foolish it appears to be. I am the hobo, who found out the hard way that the deck is stacked, the dice 'frozen', the race fixed and the wheel crooked, but there is always present that one tiny forlorn spark of hope . . .

—CLOWN EMMETT KELLY, 'WEARY WILLIE'

. . . the time for sorrow and the time for joy
. . . the time for kissing and the time for not kissing
. . . the time for saving and the time for throwing away

—ECCLESIASTES

WIN

WE'RE ON THE way home but we're not close yet. There's a week to go, eight days if you count them and I do every night. Girl is on my lap and she's asking me questions. Why is the world so bad, Win? Why isn't it more fun?

I don't have an answer she'd like to hear so I say, If you ask me the world is pretty fun. You know that we try to be funny in our acts.

What I don't say is that nothing ever changes. The clown told me about the flat circle of time and sometimes I find myself thinking about it. You want to know who the clown is? That's Valentina, she's with the show.

She told me there's nothing new under the sun which means nothing new that's good but also nothing bad. Whatever has been done will be done again. The world can't invent any more terrible things because they already exist and always have. It means that nothing is coming to save us, but also that whatever will destroy us is already here.

When Queenie heard this she made a noise. She thinks the clown talks too much. All talk and no action, is what she says. I don't know about that, but I do know Queenie does a lot of action that's for sure, and the clown, well it's true that she talks most of the time which is fine if you don't mind listening and I don't, not really.

As for the sun, it's still there it hasn't totally left but people are saying it will and the birds too. The dust is more these days and sometimes you look and can see only a blurred brightness through the haze. It's everywhere now, the dust. Sometimes it comes out, the sun I mean and those times are good. We know the sun's there, we know it persists through all of the days and all of the nights but for most people it's the light that they miss, it's the shine of it.

What I say to Girl doesn't take into account any of that. When she asks me why the world is bad, what I say back is I don't know but that she shouldn't be scared. She says, Win, why are there too many questions and never good enough answers, and all I can say to her again is that I just don't know.

When will we be home? she asks.

A few more days, I say. Not long.

Home if you want to know is an old canning factory up north. They processed all types of fruit but that was decades ago, and even though we've had it for a long time, the sign is still out front, a piece of beaten metal hanging. It has a cut-out shape of three yellow rings for pineapple: ARCADIA FRUITS.

We think about home when we're away, which is often, which is now. We've been gone for a hundred and forty-eight days and the same number of nights. We travel from place to place and look for good spots to stay and do a show or two, and for Queenie and me to do a reclamation. We're always stopping and we're always leaving, that's packing up and going to the next location. Being mostly away is what makes Arcadia even stronger in our minds. It's home for all of us and for some of us it's the only one we've had, well for one of us that is, and that's me.

WE RING THE bells at Arcadia, me and Girl. We walk on the grass and swing them through the air. The engineer found them at a garage sale, they were from a school in Victoria that had closed down. They were selling off their historical things like chalkboards and wooden desks and she found the bells, big and gold with black plastic handles. They swing heavy on the way up so you have to be careful not to lose your grip. It happened once, it went out of my hand, I was lucky it didn't land on a rock.

The bells make Girl feel stronger, she says it's because they sound the same every time. The bells help us feel where our centre is. We ring the bells to let the others know it's time for lunch or for tea. We ring them when Valentina is out as she strolls and thinks about the clown routines. We ring them so the engineer can hear from the workshop. We ring them loud so Queenie can hear wherever she is, if she's resting or reading through old papers in the boxroom. We stand on the hill and turn in circles and sometimes Girl keeps on turning and then she stops and her bell stops too. Look, Win, she says. Look how pretty the sky is. I look and yes it might be peach or even true pink. It's the colours she loves but what I see beyond is grey, I can't help it but I do try.

—

When Girl goes to the boxroom and asks to see a photograph of this or that, usually we can't find what she wants. There's no kind of system. Mostly it's photos of the elephants and when we find them we might say, Put those in a pile for Girl. But when it comes to it, when she asks to see them, they're hard to find. What I'm saying is there are piles and piles but you can't put your hand to anything you're looking for, it's more that things turn up if you wait long enough. If you ask me, you need to have an open mind and see what happens. You can't go in there expecting to find exactly what you want, that's what I'm saying.

—

But you could be in that packing room without a question in your head and find everything you might want to know as long as you weren't looking for it in the first place. What you'd learn was that a hundred years ago you could buy a lion for fifty pounds and an elephant for three hundred. How Buffalo Bill refused to travel here from America to perform, that there was no price he would say yes to. Receipts from the National Bank of India, a pink telegram addressed to 'Dearest Darling Daddles', a lifetime season ticket pressed into an album. A letter from an archbishop in Brisbane thanking the advance man Mr Murphy for the Party Ticket, saying he and the Priests had enjoyed the evening, the Show being Clean and an Education. Another letter, this one of thanks from a hospital in Ballarat for the toys sent for the unfortunate children, notes of thanks also from orphanages. Vet receipts for treatment of Rickets. A letter from father to son denying approval for a marriage, referring to the bride as That Tall Ballet Girl and threatening to cut the son off, with pleas for 'Good Sense' and accusations of an attempt to 'kill Your Mother with worry'. A framed invitation to the Official Landing of the Prince of Wales. Piles of *Reader's Digests*. Sheet music for 'Dames and Robbers', 'Baron's Entrance', 'Wedding March', 'Be a Clown', all the songs used for the old pantomimes, we don't do them anymore. Tiny notebooks where Frank was always doing his infernal calculations, that's what he called them, Queenie says. His spelling was bad but I couldn't see anything wrong with it, the main thing was you could make out what he meant. Another letter about landing the animals on return from Java, how the elephants would need blood tests and the horses weren't allowed back into Australia under any circumstances. And you know what that means, Queenie told me. Say bye-bye. A series of news articles, one about an animal tamer who suicided by lion. How he'd mentioned to the ringmaster that he was depressed on behalf of the animals, that they were unable to taste their own nature. Another about a troupe of clowns from a rival show who'd drowned in the river one New Year's Day, that's all of them. A clipping reporting a fatal fall from a tightrope act, the headline read 42 FEET AND NO NET. And finally an entire hand-written diary belonging to the youngest niece of Old Mr King, they're both dead now. I read that diary over and over and thought about how things seemed the same for her as for me all these years later. That nothing had changed. The troubles on the road and how they were always stopping, and the lists of rotten houses and meals of raw bacon cut thin and spinach floating in fat. I read it and somehow felt it was telling my life but from a time past. Queenie says the past is over but when she does, I think about all these things in the boxroom. If the past is over, what does she keep this stuff for, all these papers? That's what I'd like to know.

—

But those papers and photos are not the main thing and the bells are not the main thing either. Not the colours in the sky and not the elephants. It's the hurdy-gurdy, which is what you might call a wheel fiddle or maybe you've never heard of it. It's an instrument and Girl plays one while I have the other, mine is old and hers is new, and while she hates it, for me it's the sound I love most in the world. At first she refused to play, she said it was like a swarm of insects, that it made her feel bad, but we encouraged and pushed and now she plays, at least the drone, at least she can do that.

I was like her when I was little, I didn't like it either, the noise of the hurdies that is. It was too much, too much of everything, like having my body pulled in different directions. It came to me as an uproar, you didn't know which way to turn, you didn't know which way to look. Queenie called it a tumult because I wasn't playing right. But now I like it, which you might think strange and that's fine. I enjoy having something outside of me, something that's big which makes for balance. It's like when you stand and scream in a storm. It's like patting your head while you rub your stomach. It's like having two things in your brain and they might be opposite but you manage to let them both stay. As well as all of that, now that Girl does the drone it means I get the melodies. She's the base, the simple part it's a single note, and I do the extra bits. If the bells are to make us know our centre, the hurdy teaches us where our edges are. What might be possible in the world.

I'VE HEARD THAT to tell a good story you have to catch the person's attention right from the beginning to make them interested, so because of that I want to say by the end of this Queenie is gone and Girl is gone too. I'm sorry for this type of trick but I don't know how I can do it well otherwise. The great Russian clown Slava Polunin said, 'Sometimes I regret that I cannot hold the audience without any plot whatsoever,' and I regret that too but that's life, that's what I think because what else can we do? We have to say how it is in our own time in our own way. We have to tell our story the best we can and go on.

I WAS FOUND in a storm, that's all they told me. I can't remember for myself not when it's back to a time before my memory had even begun. I'm Win, it's short for Winnstay. You'll say what a strange name and it might be, but when you've been called something for so long it feels normal. What I mean is you become the name and it becomes you. It's the name of a street where Valentina once stayed, that was before she joined the show. They found me on the road, they say I was four or so which makes me nineteen now and that's probably all I've got to say about it to tell you the truth.

VALENTINA COMES FROM a long line of clowns, clowns and poets. Know your history, is what I've grown up hearing so I made it mine as well because I wanted one, a history that is. The Soviets produced the best clowns, they were the best in the world. Good clowns but bad cosmonauts is how Valentina puts it. Bad at freedom, good at walls. When they built their wall it worked for a time, it was a success in terms of walls but it signalled the end of freedom for most people.

Valentina's our head clown. She thinks we're all clowns but that while some of us know it most of us don't. Her grandfather was a clockmaker in Moscow, he got arrested and taken away and they never saw him again. After that her father turned clown because horology was dangerous but he found clowning difficult too. Telling jokes was an extreme sport in those days, Valentina says. It was the clowns, the funny women and men, they were the ones to care about subverting the authority of chairs and other pieces of furniture and this was how they became true revolutionaries. Clowning is more important than almost any other job apart from producing food to feed the workers and their children, that's what Valentina says too.

It was an interesting family in other ways. There was a great-aunt who was Stalin's stenographer but we don't know much about her other than she was named Vera and used to be at all his important meetings. She wrote down what they said and in the breaks she made tea and offered biscuits. It was an interesting family but they're all dead now too.

—

The great clown Polunin was the one who created the peace caravan of circuses called the MIR. They passed from Moscow to Paris through the Eastern Bloc, it was a gathering of two hundred artists and technicians. They travelled along the roads and shared ideas and gave performances about peace. They had an equal split with four groups from the west and four from the east. Valentina's father was there. He planned to string a highwire across the wall and walk it from one side to the other in a display of comradeship but it didn't happen, I don't know why.

Six weeks after the tour finished the wall came down and the clowns claimed responsibility. They said it was because of their work, they said it had been a congress. A congress of clowns. It was written in the papers that for a few months in 1989 it was the clowns who became the leaders and this was something that Valentina will be proud of until the day she dies, that's what she says. She was born another six weeks after the wall fell and it was a time when there was hope in the world.

—

There was a Chinese court jester, you could say he was a clown and he was the one person who could tell the Emperor what to do. It was at the time the other wall was being put up and hundreds of thousands of labourers had died during the building, and more would have died during the painting but this clown, he said to the Emperor, Do not paint the wall. The Emperor listened to the clown. He didn't paint the wall and it saved all of those lives.

People should listen more to clowns, I think.

WE'RE NOT LEAVING for two hours so I tell Girl we need to practise in the paddock. She complains for a bit then walks out to the wide space. She carries her hurdy, it's made of metal and slung low on her hip held with a special strap across her shoulder. The engineer made it, the hurdy that is, and says Girl holds it like a bazooka, she has her arms at full stretch when she plays. I have Valentina's one it's from her family. It's Russian and made of pear wood. It has a greased wheel and keyboard. Tangents they're called but really they're like a piano's keys.

Valentina says a hurdy-gurdy is like a medieval version of a space shuttle, that there's more than eighty moving parts. It's a mix of piano, violin and a kind of lathe. So you turn it, you turn the handle and the strings work. There's the red string, that's the trompette, it bounces off the bridge and creates a buzzy sound. The bridge is called the *chien* and it makes a fatter buzz. The *chien* is a little piece of carved wood that sits under the string. You can take it out and put it back in and I've told Girl she can't touch the dog otherwise it could get lost.

Girl plays the hurdy for me because I asked her to and she gets the red string just right. Now all she has to do on her list is: Triple somersault. Eat some pineapple. See a real star in the sky.

WE FOUND GIRL beside the road, it was past Noosa and she had on a singlet and underpants. Her hair was tangled in a knot at the back and the dirt on her face, well she put that there herself. She was smart she knew to stay away from the roads. When she saw us she came out. She ran from behind the bush and Queenie shouted, Stop! so we did.

It took two months for her to let me cut out that bit of hair at the back. She didn't want me near with the scissors before she was ready and it took longer even than that for her to laugh. Valentina had to work hard but when it finally came, Girl just stood there and it was a silent thing like she was yawning. Her eyes stayed closed too as if being happy was unsafe.

You don't have to close your eyes, we said to her.

It was strange to me that she thought laughing was somehow dangerous. We guessed she was seven and she's still very small.

We asked about her age and she said she didn't know. She couldn't tell us anything about her people, she didn't even know her own name.

WE'RE USUALLY ON the road by dawn and even though I'm not a person who enjoys an early rise, I like the way the air smells. I like how our wheels sound on the unsealed roads as we roll around rural towns and larger regional centres, the various belts that's wheat, mineral, coal. We've been away a while now like I said before and our travelling maps have the lines that Queenie has drawn, the best routes to take. The maps show other things too. It might be a black cross for a Saviour camp or a green tick for a shop or house where we can find a friend in a hurry. Other marks are a thick red line with a dot underneath, that's for a government office or police station. Queenie loves those maps, she tells us her whole life happened in bits in each circled place.

Oh, Texas in Queensland, that's where we had a broken axle and stayed a few days, yes the people were good there.

That's what made us look for the place to overwinter. Oh, Port Macquarie, that's where we got my engagement ring, it was a sapphire with two diamonds, just lovely. The macadam roads were good around there. We got married in Coffs on a Sunday, it was between shows. That's also where we got in trouble for not having permits even though you only needed one or two back then, not the dozens you had to show later. Still think it was bloody ridiculous, excuse my.

That's Queenie. She always talks that way.

—

We cross the landscape back and forth and we know the roads well. How a highway dips just after the town that has the good meat pies. How the third curve leaving the cheaper petrol town requires care because there are loose stones that can get under the tyres of an oncoming car and flip up to crack a windscreen. You could say we know the roads as well as our own bodies. That your knees can take four bad landings but not five, that's the engineer. And how thin your rotator cuffs are wearing, especially on the left-hand side which makes it best to favour the right, that's Valentina.

We try to keep to the local roads which are the backways, where you don't see another car or truck for a long time sometimes even hours. Near towns we might pass a trundle cart selling prickle pear or a bus filled with Saviours. It's drink and babies for the Saviours, they're against alcohol and for babies. We see encampments with children running, clothes lying in the open to dry and washed metalware stacked on folding tables. You can tell who they are by the signs, they tie them to tent ropes or stick them in the dirt along the way. REPENT. FREEDOM STARTS IN THE HEART. Queenie tells us to keep away from the windows when we pass, she doesn't say why but she always tells us to stay down.

—

Whenever we move through new country the engineer says a few words under her breath. Stolen from the Wiradjuri. Stolen from the Bigambul. From the Wongaibon. The Kamilaroi. You get the idea. She says it softly so Queenie doesn't hear because Queenie gives her stick for talking like that. The engineer avoids arguments she keeps it quiet and I would too, it's not worth it, arguing with Queenie I mean. But when it's just me and her, the engineer that is, she talks about how everything has changed. How it's difficult to think of these things and not be sad. That however hard we think it is for us, it's harder still for others and I know who she means by that, she means the First Nations People especially the women.

—

In the mornings when we have to get up early, sometimes I complain because I want to stay under the covers and think about love. Valentina says you have to run to it, love that is. But the mornings when I can't get up that's when Queenie says, Too bad, missy, you have to, come on, chop-chop.

I don't like it when we hurry but the reclamations can't wait. We perform and reclaim, that's all we do these days.

THERE'S THINGS TO notice on the trail with the noise and colour of different towns. Dogs that follow our truck, their eyes wild and tongues hanging, and people along the way, on the streets. They're either busy or they stop a while to talk, they lean on lampposts and point. A child being carried underneath a man's arm, he's taking her to a car. One couple arguing and another embracing. People turn to watch us as we pass, they swivel to look at the rear of our vehicles as we carry on up the way. Our truck, it's a Bedford with a sleeping section inside up top and a box for Maude, she's our pony, she's very small. There's the old Mercedes too, pulling Pet's cage, Pet's our tiger, she's a Royal Bengal. The writing on the sides of our truck says FRESH NEW LOOK, HAIRCUTS and GOLD'S FAMILY SHOW. It's a double act, Queenie says, which is one of her jokes, but I don't find it that funny to tell you the truth, none of her jokes ever are.

We stop along the way, sometimes it's a cafe or a sandwich shop or sometimes for water. A tap in a person's front garden, we knock on the door first to ask if we can fill our billy for tea, they usually say yes. Then we go about our business in the wider world, as Queenie calls it. Girl thought she said wilder and Queenie said, No love, but Valentina said, Why not? She's right. So after that we started calling the world wild and wide, and even though I haven't seen all of it, I can say so far it is exactly both those things.

—

We don't have any performances under canvas these days but it's fine, I like it best when we perform in the open, which is why the dry season is kinder to a show like ours. You can smell the dirt, it's sweet and rich but the problem is the strong-heat with big fires like the ones in '28 that burned the whole of New South Wales. They were frightening then and they still are, even if you only hear about them. We have the water tanks on top of the truck and can handpump a spottie if we need but we were lucky that time because if you think about it and I do often a handpump wouldn't help in a truly big fire because they're hell and burn the country down. I was eight or so back when we had the monster fires, that's more than ten years ago now. I was about eight and all the sky filled with black.

—

Only an elephant can stop another elephant, that's how it's always been.

What if there was only one elephant left? is what Girl said to Valentina. What would stop it then?

Our Earth is like an elephant. It's moving towards something and I can't think what could be big enough to stop it. The planet has become changed and what was old is new again. There are land wanderers once more, they roam the country and do whatever they can to stay alive. They ask for work and sleep on bed rolls in the grass on roadsides. They strip wood and beg food, it's tinkers and swaggies and bush cooks and shearers needing to get by. Travelling salespeople and tricksters and quacks selling oils and health juices.

As if a strong body will help anyone now, Queenie says, but good on them for trying. Swamp people gone off-grid with their generators, we have them as well to make our power but we aren't swampies. They stay right up north along the mangroves, we don't go there often it's too hot and too far from Arcadia.

There aren't many real shops these days. Most people don't have extra money for store-bought goods but you can find a butcher or grocer or clothier. Sometimes a bank, sometimes a library. Small towns have a haberdashery, a hardware, a lolly shop. Little stalls on wheels that get pulled by a horse or a motor of some kind. You can pretty much find what you want but sometimes you can't especially if you're a woman, that's what Queenie says.

Valentina is telling us about the Young Pioneers. We saw a billboard a while back and Girl's talking about it because she wants a uniform like that. Valentina says they remind her of the youth organisations in the Soviet Union and that people now in Russia are wishing those times were here again. She says when people start to feel nostalgia for a time that was so bad for so many, that's when we're in trouble. They should run, she says. Learn from the past.

—

When the show's over Valentina often stays behind. She goes and talks to the audience still in her costume, she'll stand beside a family if the children are upset and crying because they don't want the fun to stop. She kneels down so they can see her clown eyes and says that everything has to end. She tells them the story about her grandfather as a boy and how funny he was. That he dreamed of being a clown too. She tells them that when he grew up he made clocks but this didn't stop him from being funny, that he found he could do both at the same time. She said the policemen took him away because he made people laugh too much. They had to send him out of sight so that everything could go back to normal.

Are you a girl or a boy? sometimes children ask her.

She says she's a girl but that the face paint can make her look like a man, that sometimes she plays a man and sometimes a woman. Whatever I feel like is how I do. That's what she says.

—

After the show, before she takes off her make-up, Valentina can get quiet as if tumbling in the ring has shaken free something inside. She becomes very still and sits with her tub of cold cream balanced in three fingers and a damp face washer draped across her knee, sometimes it's a paper towel.

We should have realised all of this a long time ago, she says, back before the Koreas united, but we're stupid. We don't see what's in front of us because to do that must mean we've let it happen. It means we have to live with it or if we decide we can't, we have to do something about it, something to stop them.

No one wants to debate with her or even hear about it especially not right after a show, but for years she's talked and all that time I've listened. I've learned everything from her and I guess my brain just works the right way for it. I'm good at remembering, like elephants you could say.

—

This is how I understand it. The federal government sold the Altona grasslands for the space program with New America and New Russia. It's a joint program, they're calling it. They announced it, but they waited until after the contract was made so by then it was too late for anyone to say anything. Too late for people to gather with their anti-shuttle placards. The media were excited. NEW AGE SPACE PROGRAM and VISIONARY PACT they put on the billboards in letters as tall as Girl. Children sang about it in schools and men in offices formed fan clubs for the astronauts. Grown men made silly like boys, is what Queenie said.

I remember those billboards and the swap cards too. You could buy them in packets of bubble gum. There were forty-eight astronauts and forty-eight flavours like green tea, seaweed, iron, chalk. Children loved only six of the types, the traditional ones, they were musk and peppermint and apple, those kinds. We didn't know who could like the other ones, we just couldn't imagine who might.

—

But now they're up there again, there's another mission on. They say they're exploring but the engineer reckons it's about the space stations. A new rocket, they went up but it all turned wrong and now they're running out of oxygen. There's eight women and four men and a dog, they'll be dead in a month. Girl is especially sad for the dog. They took it, she says. It didn't say yes.

The program was to help with the climate, they said. It was to find new territory for us to live as well but anyone who's smart knows it won't be 'us' it'll be 'them' and with weapons too. There will always be weapons and anyone who thinks there won't be is just not seeing clearly. They won't stay up there forever, they'll wait until whatever happens here on Earth is finished and then they'll come back when it's safe. But being up there now and running out of oxygen would be horrible. I'd rather crack my neck in the high dive. I'd rather come off the ladder into the darkness and find myself in a never-ending fall.

I'M SITTING UP front in the Bedford with the engineer. She's our gear person. She worked with the big cats when we had them and keeps our vehicles going, that's the truck and the Mercedes. The Merc is Queenie's old car, it's black and has red leather seats, the engineer loves that car. She's the hardest worker of us all. She can make you anything and she fixes things too, and she's also a good signwriter, she can do the proper lettering in gold.

I like to sit up front and look at the maps. I study how the land falls around the coastline and how the rivers meet the sea. Our maps show the small roads, sometimes they're cut up by wheels so they're slow going and rough, especially in the dark. Even in the daytime it can be unclear and the engineer needs to shift down gears because it's hard for her to see. Sometimes it's fire-haze but mostly it's the dust. Those times Queenie talks about the spring air and how it used to come in through the car windows fresh and lovely. I've never smelled a spring air, we don't have it anymore. Instead it's the smell of salt if we're near the coast or big heat if we're inland. We have wind and rain too but neither season is a true spring and the air isn't nice these days not fresh and lovely at all, well that's my opinion anyway.

We take a day or so to get places and between shows we help all the women we can even if it means there's no time for a wade in a river or to find a mirrored shop to look at my face, Queenie says that's vain anyhow.

What could possibly be happening to your face to make you that interested in it, Miss Winnstay? It's the same face, you've got nothing new going on there.

I know my face is the same. I don't tell her I want to see how my beret looks. I got it at a sale. It's red, and even though it's for the cold I'm wearing it now. When Girl saw it she said, You look really good, Win. She said it but I want to see for myself. After Queenie mentioned that about my face, a little while later she came and sat close and gave me one of her old lipsticks.

Here, you have it. I don't need to paint it up anymore. It's called Coral Blush.

I said thank you even though I didn't much like the colour it looked pinky orange to me. I'd rather something red, something dark that makes your lips seem bigger.

In the truck, I open the small mirror above the dash and look at my eyes, that's all I can see. I do it often and to be honest

I know they haven't changed, not from before and not to now. They're the same when I wake up in the morning and the same when I'm in the front as we drive, eating stale bread and trying not to spill my water as we move along corrugated roads. They're the same as last week when it was my birthday and the same as when I started helping Queenie with the reclamations after Pearl left. The same I got in my head now when it's between a woman's legs and I have my fingers inside of her digging around. But these aren't things a person would say to Queenie. She's not the one to upset, no one can tell her a thing. She makes it sound as if she's agreeing but then goes ahead and does what she wants. She says she might be old but people can't get it over on her. She has good telomeres whatever that is. I keep things to myself and say yes when she wants me to. She's always been the boss and everybody knows it anyhow.

HOW WE PASS through difficult things is important. An unpleasant situation can be made easier by breaking things into smaller bits, it can be moments of ten or fifteen seconds. This is what Queenie taught me. Administer the ether. Hold the woman's hand. Pat her leg. Tell her it will be fine. Suggest she closes her eyes. Mention she might want to breathe deeply as if she is trying to sleep. Tell her to count the seconds.

One big rooster. Two big roosters. Three big roosters.

The thing is not to panic not you and not her because panic is when the bad things happen.

THE WOMAN

WE TRAVEL BY car, a late-century model with wide tyres. I'm the one who drives as he rests beside me. Sometimes he sleeps but he tries to keep it secret, as if to let me know he is vulnerable is too much of a risk. He turns his head towards the window and he does it to hide his closed eyes and dropped jaw but he can't fool me. He says it doesn't bring rejuvenation these days, that sleep is merely a temporary respite. He says he finds the tent meetings tiresome and the baptisms tiresome too but that as long as there is water in the rivers he has to do them. There are so many, we don't know why. You'd think there'd be a surge of godlessness rather than the opposite, which is a relentless tide of people looking for salvation. He calls the river work rebirthing souls and I suppose you could say that's what it is.

Outside, the air is the colour of tea and inside the car it's close, but we have the windows up. Additional to that, he has me keep the interior of the car clean. He was pleased when I found possum skins to further upholster the passenger seat, they warm his back well. Those skins are not legal in this state but it's comfort for him even on the most heated of days. They say we're living in a heat dome now.

When it's hot, he tells me I should take off my headdress. He calls it ridiculous. That ridiculous thing. He says he doesn't understand why I wear it. I don't tell him it makes me feel safe. It's nothing special, simply an approximation. Some pinned fabric that I stiffen up with a basic corn-starch mix. I have a skullcap, then the second piece goes on and closes around my face. The chin strap, the shoulder capelet on either side of my neck, all of it makes me pleased. He says I'm free to dress how I like but sometimes starts a fuss, usually after we've been around other people. I think he's embarrassed. By it, by me. He has other opinions about my appearance and I indulge him those. He keeps my hair cropped, does it monthly with his shears, but lets me have my cross and my one gold tooth. In the early days he'd said he would take them both but he hasn't. My tambourine, I have that too. It's one he got for me. Occasionally, when I move it, the small bells make a noise and he is displeased but it's my headdress, it's the one stubborn thing between us. I believe if he truly wanted it gone it would be, but so far I'm allowed.

—

In front of the car, the ground sweeps before us, pale as if lined with flayed bones. Ragged orbs of *Panicum effusum* tumble across the road and I keep the words in my head, repeating them to myself. Flayed bones. Ragged orbs. We're on the wide plain beside the River Dumaresq and in the distance gather flocks of long-legged birds. They stand, seemingly without purpose. They could be feeding, they could be starving, and the question has to be will they lie down and die with grace when the end comes? This is my question for them and for myself. It's my question for him, it's the question for all of us. I shift in my seat to better look out. Those birds. They can't understand how death can come at you quick or slow. That most times a person has no choice in the matter. None of us can know what's coming down the line but whether it be all at once in a heaving rush of energy or incremental and slow and you don't realise it's happening, what a joyous occasion it can be. I've seen how splendid it is, especially if a person who loves you is alongside. Waiting with patience as you see yourself out of the room. What ecstasy and comfort in that final, happy exhalation.

He speaks of a lightness of spirit when young and says that people called him protean. There were beers and racetracks and the slapping of other men's backs. He was called an eely-whacker, a cheat. He worked the three-card, the thimble and pea, and it's true the crowd could never win, but he's on the good road now. His sermons touch on this without betraying his history. He gives an explanation of how he came to be here, at this moment in time. He tells people he's not a joking man because all such exchanges are foundationally untruthful. That people hide behind humour, they use it to pass off a stinging truth as something amusing or they use it to avoid serious subjects. He tells them of his sacred mission, of the two most important matters a man could concern himself with: slaughtered babies and the evils of drink. There can be nothing funny here, he says. Nothing to laugh about. Once a person challenged him. He was a man who said all of life must be laughed at, for whatever else have we? That it is our only power to choose how to respond. This man had lost his family in an old state-operated murder and was alone in the world but had survived by finding humour in all situations. To that poor man, the Reverend said there are no jokes in the Old Testament and only one in the New. The man gave a short laugh and was dead a week later, his car run off the road into a tree.

They talk of callings but he didn't seek one, rather it came upon him. It consumed him. Whatever he was thinking before that time he has no memory of it now. He says it was a single moment when his interest in exteriority, the economic, the corporeal, the political, the social, all of it evaporated and he came to himself as if waking for the first time. He'd been at the racetrack, he'd been drinking, and lying there in the dirt beside the river he was changed. It was his moment and it was real and not one drop since.

THE WORLD HAS altered in the time he and I have been together. The infections and inquisitions, rumours of law changes and a strangled welfare system. Billionaires colonising the space stations. Our planet moving into extremity with heat events of fifty-degree days and fireflies arrived now in Tasmania. There are more households with generators than electricity running from wires. Houses made fit for other purpose, you can find mechanics and hairdressers and nail salons and medical clinics and such. Churches run from tents and sheds or garages, even the back gardens of houses.

Holidays are over, no one ordinary flies anymore, only the elite. Automobile manufactories closed long ago but some were retrofitted to produce robots that nobody can afford. There's talk of humans being replaced. People sell organs and there is talk of harvests from children, their body parts sized and sold to science or for transplants. Poor people have been selling pieces of themselves for a long time but now it's for everyone except the big rich. They're the ones making their selections from ranked parts as if grades of special meat from Old Japan. People in shantytowns and encampments and other rural areas donate, as do people living in towns, that's the regional centres with their emporiums that sell hardware and clothes and firearms. They sometimes have notices in the windows saying GOT MORE THAN U NEED? and everybody knows that means an extra kidney or retinal lens. Anything that comes in twos, one can be sold.

Then there's the opposite, which is the wealth of the capital cities with their pearl-plated cocktail bars and Russian-chef restaurants. Elaborate interiors all chrome and crystal. Statues of state-sanctioned poets and writers and composers and musicians. One is a Heldenbaritone, a singer, his statue is twice his real-life size and it towers on its plinth above the square in his birth city, where people gather and read the plaque and some even leave flowers.

This singer is not corrupt, I want to be clear about that. He's a gift to the world and as pure of heart as a newborn. He has the voice of God as described by our leader, is a man who lives even now and continues to sing. He's wheeled in a special chair onto the stage, and when the audience is seated again and quiet, once they've stopped applauding, a hoist raises his body so he can stand with one mighty hand on a platinum staff, his torso propped against a frame which is entwined with fresh flowers from the western hothouses. He sings from *Die Meistersinger von Nürnberg* or other Wagner pieces and pronounces the W as V, it's his only pretension. That, and that he performs with a single eye blackened with kohl, an affectation carried over from one stage performance or another. He wears a jewel-encrusted waistcoat and lives with his beloved wife as a guest of the government in an ivy-walled compound, the metal gates dressed with his monogram in gold. There are servants and silk bedlinen and whatever food they desire can be flown in, and they come and go as they please—it's not like you're thinking, they are free.

For the rest of us, internet service is glitchy and sometimes they switch it off and this makes people angry because what can they do with their opinions then? Water and electricity are sporadic and the skyfarming is not working and the seedbanks at each pole, we haven't read about them in a while.

Smugglers run their grog and pharma trades along the thinning rivers and some years the waterways die only to come back to life after the dumped rain masses up north. Harvests rot in the wet, these cyclonic storms are new, and the rain projects and cloud seeding—all of it has failed. They can't germinate clouds when they're dying or gone and what we see above these days is mostly uncloud. What we have now is the sky-haze from the dust, orange in colour, it's stuck here just like us. We aren't rich enough to flee, we've been left to whatever they have planned. Some say it will be a series of virus events but others believe there's no schedule, that we're all falling into nothing. You see, the whole planet is sick and humanity is the disease.

WHAT'S FOR LUNCH do you think? he asks and I say I don't know, but my meaning is I don't care. We're on our way to the next place and the meal they serve is likely to be a sandwich or a plate of sausage and potato, something simple. He's fine with that, he always is, I don't know why he wonders.

Don't you find yourself hungry? he asks and I don't reply. He knows this too and it's an irritation that he returns to it.

They don't love me, he says, sitting there beside me on his possum skins. They don't come for me anymore. It's those new churches and young preachers, showmen they are, telling people how to feel. Driving around in expensive cars like music celebrities. Their gold chains, leather jackets, some of them with piercings and split tongues, I've heard tell.

They come for you. Of course they do, I say.

You hear anything about split tongues?

I say I don't. I wish he'd quieten but he doesn't.

Hundreds of dollars for shoes! The people, they listen to me, I know it. They stamp and shout but at the end I'm empty, not filled with light as I was before. I wish those days were still with me. I can't explain what's happened but I don't know where that light has gone.

I don't say anything.

They aren't interested in understanding, he goes on. They want to be told how to feel. He lifts a hand to the window. It's too late. Humans can only be humans, they can't be any other way.

I hit the indicator, shift down a gear and then another and we turn into an intersecting road. There's gravel under the wheels as we draw into the encampment. Now, the welcoming party, a gathering of men from the community standing with their sons in front, hands clasped in preparation to greet us. To say, Welcome, Reverend Francis Abernathy Goldfinch Jones. Welcome to our camp, praise the Lord.

—

Me? I have no name these days, I am called Sister. He found me on the picket line, it was a while back. I was a student of nursing when I heard about the clinic protests so I went and joined. It was a day of shouting and pushing. At the end of it he came to me and asked me to go with him and we've been together since that time, though once he said he wasn't yet sure whether he would keep me.

He took me from there and we travelled and I listened to his words. I read as we went, different things, articles he gave me and he changed my progressive thinking, wrong thinking he called it. Facts and figures I've always had a good brain for. I read or hear a thing and remember it well, such as how this area we're in now is famed for a cave that produces a particular type of liquid on its walls that people like to taste. I'll admit to curiosity, it's not a sin to want to know things.

—

The tent is filling with people of all categories as we walk through. The walls they've lined with painted sheets with the words of God written in big letters, a quotation from the Bible: AND HE WILL MAKE STRAIGHT YOUR PATHS. The tent is a green top with a white cross stitched into the roof. You look up and there it is, above all of our heads, it lifts in the breeze. I check they have the loudspeakers, that they're on the poles and connected. His voice is weaker these days, he needs the amplification.

We're outside now. A charity group has brought in a water point and there are portable toilets and an outdoor kitchen under a shade cloth. The land around us is wracked by heat. Fields mostly bare but for scraps of grass tree. There hasn't been a solid rain, not for a long time. The rising of hot air, the aridity that flattens a person's face. What's in the air these days is mostly despair but I watch people and try to gauge their emotions. I'm not a mind-reader, even though he taught me the tells. We practised once or twice but it was too hard for me.

Merchants, landowners and businessmen come with their families to hear the sermons. There are children sitting cross-legged on straw mats at the front, watched over by women who sit in a half-ring around them. The very young are restless, they hold little wooden figures painted yellow or blue but dolls won't take their minds off their empty bellies, dolls won't help, they never have.

Adults are dressed in old-fashioned clothes, some wear pinafores or shirts, their collars well pressed. Most are white and many are men and there's a shifty yearning in their demeanours as they line the walls at the sides of the tent, arms crossed and heads lowered. They wait as if ready to be filled and by the end they will be on their knees sobbing. They're seeking something specific which is for their flaw to be named in front of all. To have someone see them. To tell them they are indeed terrible but that despite all of it, they're human and they're loved.

Everyone knows there is wrong in them. To start with, a person doesn't want it to be apparent and they work hard to keep it hidden, but then comes a time when tiredness and hunger threaten to overwhelm. The knocks become too many and gather to form something crushing, and it's then that we want to lay ourselves down in front of someone strong, someone who we can be sure sees us.

They come to him and he can identify their weakness which is always rooted in pain. He understands where it sits in their bodies, can guess from whom it originated or to whom in their lives it's attached, present or past. Mother, father, sibling, partner, child. It's one of these, sometimes more than one, and there is accretion with time. In this world, no one is untouched.

He's learned that when someone knows you've seen their wrong yet are happy to look them full in the face, it's proof that you will accept that person, love them even knowing the flaw. It's the most powerful act of all. See the badness, see the weakness, see the quality that frightens and not turn away. Love them still, as a parent is meant to a child, as so many parents don't. They don't see, they don't understand. Yes, his words keep them coming, to hear those small mentions of forgiveness and absolution, but it's the belief—the hope—that the words, the seeing, can make things better.

—

We're in the back now behind the curtain, he's getting ready. I'm in front of him, kneeling to tie his laces. It makes him angry, the sight of me down there. I focus on the black-and-white wingtips with the ripple sole, they're a little formal but never mind, these people won't notice his shoes. All they care about is their small businesses, their land, their bellies. Their sexual perversions and children's illnesses. Their quest to be understood.

I make sure he has a clean shirt. He takes pride in his appearance still. Suit coat in summer and full-length rabbit fur in winter, I notice he pulls it on earlier these days. Whether it's the shifting chill that comes to inhabit ageing bones, or some need for protection, for a type of armour, I cannot know. It's probably both as most things are.

My hands are on his ankle now. He doesn't like me fussing with his socks so he moves his foot, shakes it to the side.

That's enough, he says. I'm ready.

—

Each meeting I watch him from the back and he has me report to him later. How he pauses at this or that moment. My notes record when he rocks and other times moans.

I do not hug myself, he tells me. That's absurd.

Well, they like it, I say, and then he says, That's true. Sweet heck, they really do.

The meetings remind him of the boxing ring, he says. There was a time he lived in the city, he worked as a butcher by day and boxer at night. He could still hit a man on the jaw and drop him even now, he's sure of that, but I doubt it—I've seen how weak his body has become. He thinks I don't watch him down at the river as he washes. How thin his torso has grown.

And once he's done, in the tents, on the stage, it's in the minutes that follow that the crowd presses forward to talk, to touch. They want to hold his feet, his hands, his shoulders. Sometimes, he counsels one or two of them before I manage to steer him away.

Enough, I say to them. Can't you see he's finished?

He tells me he has no memory of what he says. It's something that happens, that passes through him, and he knows it for what it is: the Almighty. He likes to pretend that the words come to him in the moment but I know he has thought about his topics and worked out some of what he will say, that he's even written parts of his speeches down. He chooses the words—not the other way around—and while they do come out hot, it's not without thought.

For me it's different. I wait for my words, and it might be in the night or when out in nature, always when I'm alone but sometimes, like earlier, when I'm driving and he is dozing.

Ragged orbs. Long-legg'd birds.

I write the words down, manage to scribble them into the small book I carry.

It could be in a wide field when I'm allowed a moment to contemplate, and having gone out there with a chance to realise again how wrong the colour of the sky or how vibrant the green of a single trembling leaf. When the words arrive I must be ready to record them, I must be ready otherwise they'll pass right through me and leave. They don't wait so I must be ready and try to write them down. When this happens, I'm filled with something close to beauty and a piercing, almost-painful tenderness. Unlike his, my words are private. I don't speak them to anyone, I don't allow them any light.

—

He walks to the front, past the curtain. There is a wave of heat coming off them, from the people waiting. His back straightens and I get in my seat.

He will start with matters of the pelvic zone.

—

Well, hello everyone. How have you kept these last few months?

I sit up the back in my elevated chair. It's made of metal with wooden slat seating and allows me a good view. We found it at a tennis court and went back later that night to liberate it. You can watch me, he said at the time. You can give me notes on my speeches. I told him it wasn't my place to critique but he had his way, he always does.

To the crowd he starts by saying that it appears being good, being right, is a dangerous thing these days.

They laugh at this.

Ridiculous, isn't it? To be punished for correct thinking.

He begins with the babies. He tells his stories, all of them general at the beginning. He builds a picture. Introduces character. Says that using narrative is the best way to make people listen. They like to follow along, hear the story. They invest in the telling. He speaks his anecdotes then moves to specifics.

He says that people need to be suspicious of those who have simple solutions for complicated problems. They might seem friendly. Yes, they'll listen and be sympathetic, but people must remember that anything can be made normal. Infanticide was normal. Slavery. Stoning women for adultery, all was seen as normal.

He tells the crowd that he wants them to join him and become saviours of the precious unborn. He asks them to pray for the discarded souls. He wants them to do it that night as they lie down to sleep. They might be in a tent or car or building of their own.

It doesn't matter where you are, he says. What's important is you think about it carefully and do what you can to stop it. Violence may be necessary. Imagine. A baby lying in the very place it should be safest. No bleach to drink, no power sockets. And who kills it? The mother.

A foetus doesn't need to have a beating heart to be alive, is what he believes and he says that now. We have to acknowledge its human potentiality, whether it's at the beginning and has a nub of cardiac nerves spitting out electricity or if there are fingernails or hair. These things don't matter. What does matter, and it matters greatly, is that from the moment the spermatozoon pushes into the ovum and fertilises it, once that merged cell divides and journeys along the fallopian tube, even before implantation, that is human life. And is not each human sperm and human ovum a living human cell, not dead? The dead don't reproduce, no sir they do not.

A voice is coming now, it's a woman's and she's shouting. I lift a hand to my eyes. The lights are too bright I need one of those visors. I look around and there she is. Standing, yelling across the heads of the others gathered.

You speak of the sanctity of life? You're talking about the unborn and men's rights to procreate, but you're not talking about me. Not about the women. What of our lives?

She doesn't manage to say anything else because now she's being dragged away by the organisers. They have her by the arms, they're carrying her from the tent. They're being rough and her head taps one of the poles on the way out. Her voice is cut short.

He looks to the back, where I perch. I lift a hand. It is alright.

He continues. He apologises for the interruption. Of course they want to stop us, he says. He warns about the euphemisms. 'Interruption of gestation before viability.' 'Remedy for irregularity.' 'Suppression of a neonate.' As he talks, I scan the crowd. I'm alert to people who may not be of like thinking. Someone who might come as a spy, arriving with their minds already made, closed to our way but fully open to the murder of babies. These people are dangerous and we don't have time for them.

At eighteen minutes, I begin my descent. I come down from the high chair, I'm on the ground and moving forward, it's time to finish. We don't spend long at each place. He doesn't have the energy he used to. I can hear it in his voice, there's a slowing.

He's holding on to the lectern. He's talking about the abortionists. Asking the crowd for their help. Do they know people who do this abominable work? He stands in silence. Then repeats: Have you heard of such a person?

I reach the front, where people are standing. I try to push them back but men surge towards him.

Yes, they shout. We know them. There's a man by the old paper mill. There's an ex-nurse up in Rockhampton. Women stand at their seats and children are crying and it's a horrendous chaos.

I'm there now, I'm beside him. An older woman is trying to speak to him through her tears. She sees me and clutches my arm. A man is holding out his hand to the Reverend, beckoning. A child grips my leg, urine leaking from its nappy. Women hold infants aloft, trying to give them to him. This is how it ends each time, in a melee. He needn't worry about numbers. The new churches can't accommodate everyone. There are plenty of souls still available, such as this writhing mass of humans, all of them trying to be heard, all of them trying to be seen. To matter.

—

I find her outside. She's sitting on the ground, hand to head with a bruise forming around one eye. I give her a plate of food and she starts to weep.

I kneel beside her, I have a handkerchief. It's clean, I say, and she takes it.

She thanks me, she reaches out to me and I hold her hand. I open her fingers and look there. I say to her, Everything will be fine, don't worry, you will be well. I let go of her before he wonders where I am.

—

Where were you? he asks. Did you take the testimonies? Go now, I want to know if any one of them is sensible. I stand at the tent flap. I let the people talk to me but keep my eyes on him. Most of the stories are empty, there's nothing to write down. I go to him and sit at his feet. He tells me that his back aches, how it comes and goes but these days is making him nauseous. He asks the attendant nearby to fetch a piece of bread or a cracker.

Perhaps if I eat something, he says.

I say it might help.

They don't really love me. Not me.

I don't know what more you expect, I say. They come to listen, they come in numbers. Look at them all out there, wanting to be heard by you.

He sits with his eyes closed and before I can stop them, the words are out.

You seem tired, I say.

He swings his arm across his body and on the return strikes my cheek. I fall to the side.

He leans over me.

I'm never tired, he says. It's never that.

The boy comes back with bread and cheese. The Reverend takes it from him and thanks him.

Who bakes this? It's very good.

My sister, I hear the boy say. I'm still lying on my side. I've learned it's best not to rise too rapidly. He abhors any sign of strength, it just makes things worse.

What are you standing there for? he says to the boy. Help her up. And bring more bread, it's very good. Bring it out to the car.

He goes outside and I follow.

WIN

IT USED TO be called the quickening when a foetus started to move, Queenie says. You could put your hands on the belly and feel it shift under your fingers, stretching its muscles. This is the stage when what is growing becomes real for the mothers and they love to know it, it's a time of joy. As long as it is a time of joy. For the ones who want to be mothers.

People used to do it back when she was younger. People have always done it. The rich could go to proper doctors, they chewed mints to make their breath nice and kept their hands clean and soft, the doctors I mean. Sometimes you have to extract the foetus piecemeal and if you don't know what that is you shouldn't ask and definitely I'd say don't search the internet, if you still have any that is.

Some men kill people who do it, who do reclamations. I ask why men get so bad, how they turn to cruel so quickly, but

Queenie says, Well, women can be cruel too, it's true that it's yumans not genders, and she says yumans with a y, that's how she says it.

This is one thing that is simple, she goes on. We have to think of the women first. We have to help them. Men protect each other so we women have to do the same. It's not their business anyway, they should keep their noses out of it, oh yes they should.

She tells me about hers. She says the room stank with the smell of burning.

It was bloody awful, excuse my. A small window, it had those louvred glass panels, they were cracked open a bit but still the smoke in my nostrils, well I'll never forget that. They put me on a table in the kitchen. Lie down, the woman said, so I did. The pattern of the laminex, red-flecked it was, and I found myself there like a piece of meat.

There was a man who smelled bad too, his hot breath on my thigh, and the woman was there to help but she could not be even a little bit kind. My husband, he sat outside. It was him who brought me to that place. Him who insisted it wasn't the right time, that we take care of the problem, but it was the opposite of that, there was no care in any of it. He brought me there as if I was a dog to be dealt with by a veterinarian.

I remember the woman went to the door and asked for him to help, to come and hold me down.

My husband came to where I was on the table. He looked down at me with his hateful face and took my shoulders. He leaned on them, holding me while the woman pressed my hips. After, my husband asked for it to be put into a jar, he said it was a reminder.

Queenie showed it to me, she showed me her baby in a jar, that's what she called it, her baby. She let me hold it and floating inside it's the size of a plum. It has fingernails just started, also arms and legs. I wanted to hold it up to the window, to the light but knew she wouldn't let me because already her hands were reaching for it and she took it away. She keeps it in a box, it has velvet lining, and the box stays in a bag made of thick cloth. She's carried that jar for a long time, it could be sixty years or more.

Why did you keep it? I asked and she said she couldn't bear not knowing where her boy was. That it would send her mad, not to know.

Why do you do it to other women then?

Because they ask me to. She put the jar back in the box and that was that.

She told me there's no pain because the brains aren't finished. That their bodies aren't finished either so how could they ever hope to live outside of the woman? She said all of this and I knew she was telling the truth but what I wanted to say was: They don't need to come outside the woman's body. They can stay inside and everything will be alright.

When I say I can't think of a worse thing to do to a person Queenie says, Oh, there are worse things and I hope you never learn about any of them.

I left that place with his hand on my elbow, she goes on. I fell into fever and infection and almost left myself and it was only the kindness of the woman next door that helped me through. The thing is that many men are bad and even when they're not bad they're not that good either, she says. They should be better but no one can force them so they do what they want. The jar was to remind me, that's what he said. To keep me thinking straight. He gave me my baby to keep in a jar but what it did was make me hate him. He was cruel after that, he was many times cruel, and one night accused me of something so terrible I can't even say the words. That was it, that was the end. I waited till he was asleep and gave him a slice on the neck and ran away into the night. That's it, that's all, go on judge me if you like I don't care.

She continues.

I'll tell you another story. After my father died, a man came to our door asking for cash money. He said we owed him and it was a lot, far more than my mother had to give. I remember her crying and my older brother trying to make her stop. He was fifteen and I was ten. I couldn't understand why they were upset.

We don't have the money, I said once the man had gone. There's nothing he can do.

My mother turned to me. I expected her to be angry but not who she was going to be angry with, which was me. She told me that this man could ask for me, that he could try to take me.

I laughed. I didn't see what she meant.

My brother was weak, he didn't know what to do but I did. When that man came back I told him he'd better leave us alone, that we didn't have the money and if he liked he could go and dig up my father's body and check his pockets because that was the only place he'd have a chance of finding coin. I said I'd spoken to my schoolteacher and she had one brother who was a lawman and another who was police. I told him my teacher said she would help and that her brothers would help too.

Standing in the doorway the man called me a tough cookie and what I learned that day is that you can't rely on others to do the right thing, not even your own mother. I believe she might have let him take me, that man.

Of course I hadn't told my teacher any of it. She hated me, she looked down on us because we were poor. But I learned that day that lies can be helpful and I also learned that people will underestimate you every single time. I thought it was because the man at the door saw me as too young but I have since come to realise that he saw me as too female.

—

Women got tired of men hurting them. They wanted to burn things down. Too many girls and women locked up, shut in rooms, put underground. When you've heard about those places as often as Queenie has, it changes you. It was enough, she decided. The time for talk was over. We can get rid of the babies is what she said. See how they like that. She was already doing them, the reclamations that is. But more women came, more women couldn't keep what was growing inside them. More women thought it was enough.

People are worried about climate change, they're worried about neoliberalism and creeping fascism, but what they should be worried about is women. That's what Queenie says too.

In the end, men want women and women want safety. That's it, that's the whole problem, she says. We're not here to debate. Women have tried the other ways but none of them work, and the world's men don't do anything so it's up to us. We have to be tough, we have to be strong. That's the most important thing, she said. No more softly-softly.

I DON'T THINK it's the most important thing but I don't tell Queenie that. I don't tell her I think love is important. Girl is learning to be tough, which I guess is good, Queenie says it is, but Girl also has a soft side. She tells us about her good dreams, one was of a bear who sat at a table and ate pieces of pineapple. That's all it did, it was very funny, she said. We should do that in the show, she went on, but Valentina said, Where will we find pineapple, it's all gone? Where will we find a bear these days, and anyway they stink.

It's not the bear's fault, Girl said. Nobody's perfect.

She doesn't like it when the others laugh. Those are the times she comes and sits on my lap and I tell her not to mind them. I say that she has to be stronger and that's when she says, But I'm strong already Win and she shows me her arm, she bends it and pops a tiny muscle.

We can find some can't we, Win? We can find pineapple?

I say we can try even though I know there's none left, not on the farms and not in the shops. It's funny how she can love something she's never had but she does and I don't want to disappoint her any more than I have to.

—

There were no pineapples in Soviet Russia, or very rarely, Valentina says. She tells about her father touring with the show in the Far East and they were in a port town that overlooked a river. One day a freighter carrying tonnes of the fruit from Vietnam got stranded. The pineapples started to rot so there was nothing to do but give them to the shops to sell. This was a time when to buy milk you needed to be sick and have a note from your doctor. Suddenly there were pineapples everywhere, and they were cheap and you could find them in the windows of bookshops even. Children were having them for lunch in sandwiches each day at school. Valentina's father had never tasted pineapple before, he said it was like eating sunshine. Then they all got used up and that was the end of it.

And now it's the same in this country.

Pineapples. They were here for a long time and then one day, they weren't.

—

Pineapple could cause miscarriage because it contained bromelain which made contractions in the uterus. It softened the cervix and they say you took a little with honey on a few mornings in a row or had to eat ten of them at once or two to three whole per day. Of course different people say different things, it's hard to know what's real, so even if you could find them it's probably best not to try it I wouldn't if I were you. The other thing is it could shred the flesh in your mouth, so that while you were eating sunshine, it was also eating you. I haven't told Girl any of this, I'm keeping it to myself. I want her to hear only the nice things about pineapples.

—

The women come to us when their pessaries and poultices and herbs don't work, when their attempts to crush and expel fail. They're made pregnant against their will, they have too many children already. Their pills if they can get them are thrown away or condoms pulled off in the dark it's a never-ending thing. These days, they can't get Mif+Mis, they can't deal with it straight after and then soon it's too late.

We have lots of rules. Don't give receipts, don't ask women to bring pads. We call it returning a missed period, we don't call it what it is, always something else as if using other words means we aren't doing what we really are. Queenie isn't ashamed she says it's easier to use those other words. She puts music on to help as well. I want to ask her if we can listen to something different but I don't want to make her cross, she's old and tired and sometimes she gets snappy. Things are worse when Queenie gets snappy.

—

When we're doing reclamations, the smell can be of sweat, especially if the woman has walked a way to get there, but even when they come by car and it's the coldest of days, that smell of perspiration is common. Queenie says she thinks of that particular odour as one of bravery. It's of a body that knows fear but is still in action, still moving forward. Not frozen, not given up. It shows the woman is upset, that she's in a state she doesn't want but that she needs for it to be fixed. The sweat will stop once it's over, once everything is done.

Sometimes women wear perfume, it can be cheap or expensive, but even so you can smell the sweat, you can smell the other body odours too especially the most intimate ones. They apologise for not having washed and one said sorry for not having shaved and another for not brushing her hair but Queenie pats their legs—no more than one big rooster—and says, Now pet, enough of that, it's not important. Let's get you sorted and on your way.

I never spent a lot of time wondering about much of it to tell you the truth. How the women sometimes drive a car but mostly arrive on bicycle or by foot. They appear around bends in lanes, they might tramp eight kilometres from the train and arrive with their faces flushed. Their bodies are long and thin or short and round, that's all types, and they're some young, some middle and some old, most of them tired and none of them excited. They come all months wherever the show is pitched and sometimes even at Arcadia, they come there too. They have their hair done or just the other and then it's out into the day or night. They disappear and take themselves back to wherever they came from.

A nice haircut sorts them out, Queenie used to say, and for a long time I believed her.

—

You might wonder where we find the women or how they find us. Well, they're from the towns and they're from the land. We find them in laundromats and beauty salons and supermarkets, all the places women go, that's where we leave our flyers. We visit hairdressers and cake shops, we leave some at hotels too. We give them to publican wives because they're on the down-low and we give them to female nurses in clinics, and female teachers too. Old women because they know younger women. Flyers that say TRIMS & PERMS, MAKE A BOOKING WITH FRESH LOOKS and then our phone number. Sometimes we put an advertisement in local newspapers and it's the word

'FRESH' that's important because women have learned what it means, they've passed it along. We're doing more reclamations these days and Queenie says it's a good thing. Get rid of men's children, she says. Why not? We should get rid of the future men too.

—

Queenie's talking about the new vouchers which are FREE SHAVE. We pass them out to the special customers, these are the ones Queenie decides should bring their husbands or boyfriends or sometimes it's their fathers for a cut. We don't give out many and only when she's certain. She'll speak to the woman, she'll find out what's going on, then say, Bring him for a shave why don't you?

We have to be careful. Queenie's heard stories about men with dogs and drones. They hunt girls and women who've run away and they might hunt us too.

She's careful not to say those things in front of Girl which I get I really do, but sometimes I wish she wouldn't say them in front of me.

QUEENIE'S TOLD ME to find Girl, this is back at Arcadia, before we came away. I'm looking but she isn't around so I go to the barn and then to the workshop. I hear a noise from behind a drop-cloth, it's a sheet fixed to the top of something large. Before I can look she appears from behind another screen across the way. She steps out just like that.

Come over here, she says. It's the secret.

I go towards an old section of canvas as she disappears behind it. On a shelf nearby I see the suitcases, it's one of her projects, the engineer that is. A circus with animals and performers, she made them from twisted wire and bits of cloth and corks cut into shapes. She spent a long time on it and used to make shows for me when I was little. I remember her on the floor, she had special pads for kneeling. This was in the winter and she'd stay there for hours, for as long as I wanted, hunched over the cork-and-wire show. Later, there was a little mechanical seal, it was white with green spots, it had wires from its midsection and a tail and flippers. It swam against a rock when you turned the crank. I loved that seal more than anything for a time.

On her bench nearby, a pair of pliers and something else like scissors and white plastic shapes fitted together, she calls it a prototype.

I push the canvas to the side and step through and of course it's dark in there, we're up against one of the walls and there's no skylight. It takes a moment for me to see. In front is a big metal cage and Girl is inside of it and it looks like a cat. She's up high on all fours, her body horizontal inside the frame, her feet and hands on pedals. The outline of her is shown by her white top and yellow shorts, and around the whole of her, fitting her, is an irregular metal structure in the shape of a lion. I'm too close to see the whole of it but I make out a head and inside her own face emerges, small and excited as she hovers, suspended. Her face is tipped up at me and she's smiling.

Does it work yet? I'm trying not to laugh but it's not mockery, it's amazement.

Not yet but she's going to make them move, she tells me. I'll be able to run in mine but hers is slower so she can only walk. I ask what the engineer's is but she won't tell me.

That's her surprise, she says. This one's mine so I can show you.

She climbs out and comes to stand near me.

I want to go inside it myself. I want to be inside the lion.

After she skips away, after she skips out of the workshop, I stay in there a few minutes more. She might call it a surprise but if you think about it there's no surprise in a girl wanting to climb inside a metal animal, wanting to be in there, to stay in there a while.

—

The prototype on the workbench has numbers written on the plastic but the engineer calls it Jaws and I guess you could say it's a safety device. It sits inside the woman, it has a mechanism that shreds anything that goes in, it might be a finger or something else. It has barbs that dig in and catch when the man tries to take it out, the engineer told me. You know, his penis, she said. It's like a condom. She saw that I didn't really know what that was so she explained that to me as well.

It stays on and he can't get it off. He needs to go to a doctor to remove it which will be evidence of what happened, she said.

We figure it's better than the belts we sometimes see women wearing, that's metal belts the engineer has to unlock when they come for a reclamation. The belts don't really work. They can make men enraged, make them even more violent but Jaws is invisible until it isn't. Until it shows its teeth. That's how Queenie puts it. She calls it smart, she calls it genius, although the engineer said it wasn't her idea, that she read about it somewhere she can't remember where.

We can sell them to the women, Queenie said.

The engineer told her that was possible but she hadn't made it to sell.

Why did you bother then?

For them, the engineer said and pointed at me. One for her and one for the little one too. For when the time comes.

WE'RE STOPPED ON the side of the road. It always happens, I can't say how many times something goes wrong with one of the vehicles, it's the way of the show. We're pulling over because of something with the axle or another thing with the tyres and if it's not the truck it's the car.

Last time we broke down, Queenie told me and Girl to ask at a house further along the way to see if they had any eggs for sale but I didn't want to.

Just go, Missy, she said. It was too hot I said and I was tired. Queenie got cross with me and Girl ended up going by herself.

Queenie said, If anything happens to her, Win, I swear.

I told her I didn't care but afterwards I felt bad because of course I do, I care.

THE ENGINEER IS on her back, she's under the front of the Bedford, lying on the road with her sleeves rolled up and her tattoos showing. She's reaching up and clanking underneath so I go to help, she can always use a hand. She hears me arrive and says, Look here, and I know what she's doing, she's teaching me, like she's taught me about other things. Look at this, she sometimes says in her workroom, and shows me her metalwork, it might be the head of a giraffe or an articulated insect antenna painted a delicate silver. Look at this, she says. Do you like it?

Girl is over by Pet's cage. The engineer has rigged up an umbrella, we close it when we're on the move and tie across the cloth and it's Girl's job to open them both when we're stopped so Pet can get shade and a good breeze. Girl knows to keep her hands well away from the cage door, she understands that even though Pet seems calm and sleepy she will bite her if she can.

What does she eat? she asked me recently.

The engineer feeds her, she has meat.

But when?

It's when you're asleep, very early or very late.

Is it kangaroos? Girl asks and I say, Yes. It's kangaroos.

—

We have long days to travel before we get to Whiteacre for a show, then it's a reclamation and then we're due at Riverside. Another woman and on home soon after that. We're looking forward to it, to being back at Arcadia, but I look at the sky and there's white through the trees and I know there'll be storming before then. We're at the end of the season and bad weather makes the roads slow. Before the wet there are dust clouds and after it's the rain and then the mud and that's when our wheels get heavy and stop. Sometimes it can feel as if our tyres are spinning in place and we aren't getting anywhere. Sometimes it can feel as if we're going backwards.

—

We drive two hours and we pass a lot of places. There's a Supa Sundaes and dry-looking wetlands and after that an Exotic Fruit Garden.

They wouldn't have any, would they? I call back.

No, Queenie says. They're finished, you know that.

Cattle King, golf club, Caltex, show society.

Ask when she wants to stop, the engineer says, and I call again to the back, to Queenie where she's holding the bag in her lap, her jar in a box, she never goes anywhere without it.

I say, Shall we stop? She nods and I say yes to the engineer.

Up ahead there's a shack with people sitting out front so I grab the edge of the cabin and go further into the dark, back to where Girl and Queenie are. Queenie is talking about the dentist and Girl is saying she doesn't want to, she doesn't want to go. She doesn't want anyone to look in her mouth.

Don't you want to be able to chew properly? Queenie asks. And smile and have them not be broken? You could have lollies then.

Girl says, Maybe for lollies, and Queenie says, Right. We'll take you after Riverside.

—

At noon we're having our meal but Girl isn't eating, she's upset. We've been talking of the old days when the vehicles were pulled by horses and even the elephants and she doesn't believe it, she says I'm a liar. Eat your food, I tell her.

I take my tea and move away, but any time I look over she's watching me. Before we get on the road again she comes and says sorry and I let her on my lap and play with her hair and she tells me, Win, I love you. I say to her it's fine, that she's not to worry. I tell her that I never get angry when she says those things. She grabs my chin and pushes my nose to hers and waits. Her eyes are hard and she's almost crying so that's when I say, Alright. I love you too.

SOME PEOPLE THINK it's a conscience that separates us from the animals but it's laughter, that's what Valentina says. With applause, well anyone can put two hands together and bang them but you can't help laughter coming, not when it's real. People who stopped clapping too soon were taken from Stalin's auditoriums and shot outside and then, because he thought he was truly comic, any people who stopped laughing at his jokes too quickly were taken out and shot as well. We don't have auditoriums and we don't have Stalin and they might not be shooting us yet but still we die, that part hasn't changed. You'd think the government would protect women and children from being hurt, it's half the population, but they don't care as long as there's enough of us left, that we don't all disappear. But they're bringing artificial wombs soon and that'll be the end of us, that will really be the end.

IT'S THE NEXT morning. We leave Valentina and Girl behind because she's too little and Valentina's no good in a fight. We drive out in the truck, we're heading east. We pass a cemetery, a district hospital, a glasshouse complex that grows tomatoes. We're on the road for almost an hour when we see a manure stall and Queenie calls from the back, We're close. Go on five more, there's a clearing to the left, it's after that.

The engineer says alright and in less than ten minutes we're there and off the road at a rest stop, near where the rivers become braided. It's never really rest at the rest stops, not for us it isn't.

Rubbish bins and toilets and taps for water. No one else parked which you'd think is good but even so, we've done this with families eating their sandwiches at a picnic table nearby and truckies sleeping in their cabs. They don't notice anything, it's like Queenie says. People only care about their own business until they want to get stuck into yours, that is. They don't see and they don't care, she says. All they can think of is their own bloody problems, excuse my.

We park under a tree. The engineer gets out to unload the chairs and card table. She sets out cups and biscuits and the thermos. I climb in back to where Queenie is reaching for the tub. I help her with it and then set up the barber chair and get the towels ready. We heat water on the stove and once everything's ready, we get out at the side door. We sit and wait, the phone on the table in front of us. We're not there even a few minutes, it hasn't been very long, and I'm about to suggest we play a hand of cards when there's the sound of a car approaching, make that more than one, it's two. Dual-cab utes with men inside, their windows open and arms holding doors. Men leaning out with more sitting in the back trays, they have guns sticking up between their legs.

Oh my, Queenie says. She stands and grabs her cane, she's quick about it and the engineer stands too. She opens her jacket, she has a holster underneath.

Tub, the engineer says to me, and she and Queenie start walking to the cars which are parking now. Men are opening doors and jumping down, they're raising dust, they're moving fast.

I go through the curtain into the truck to put the tub away in the hidden spot, then go back out to see what's happening. Queenie and the engineer are over with the men. There's eight of them, they're big, all of them tall like the engineer. I can't hear but it's one man, he's doing the talking, he's waving his hands in the air. He doesn't have a gun but the others do, they're standing around, their weapons look like semis but I see one or two rifles.

Now Queenie's talking and the men listen but their faces are closed. One of them takes a step forward but the first man puts a hand out, he stops him. Queenie keeps talking, she'll be doing her lying, saying that we don't know anything. That they've got the wrong people. She'll tell them she knows exactly who they're after but that they've moved their operations west. All the excuses, every single one. I heard her two years ago when a police officer stopped our truck on the highway. They said they'd heard something about us. They searched the truck with Queenie following them all the while, telling her lies.

You think somebody of my age is doing that? Shame on you. What would your mother say?

She and the engineer are walking back. They seem normal and Queenie's chin is up. She doesn't let anyone scare her. When they reach me she says, Come on, Win, we're leaving. We pack the truck down and climb into our seats and the men escort us twenty kilometres down the road. They sound their horns and we look behind to see them turning. They head in the opposite direction, they're leaving us to continue by ourselves.

Queenie is very quiet all the way back. She was going to show me how to do the dispatch and I'm glad it didn't happen.

I don't want to give anyone a free shave. I don't want to learn it and I don't want to do it, not to anyone.

—

It's a recent idea. Queenie calls it a dispatch, a community service. It's after we've noticed certain things about a woman or a girl, that's Queenie, she's the one who notices. A bruise on the arm it might be, or an eye that's gone the wrong colour. She said there used to be training in the cities, they told hairdressers how to spot women who were being hurt but that was years ago. Men stopped it, they said it was ridiculous. Queenie says she doesn't need training, that she's always been able to know a beater and she's good at talking to them, the women that is. She waits for them to say the words, she does it without leading them because she has to make certain. Then the man comes and brings a voucher. He sits in the chair and Queenie ties a towel around his neck and he thinks he's having a close shave, and it is close but it's not a shave, it's not that at all.

She tells me I need to learn how to do the free shave. She says it'll be easy. They close their eyes and relax and wait for what's coming next, which they think is a smooth chin. Sometimes they smile and imagine how they'll be able to go and sweet-talk some woman or girl.

She looks at me. These are bad people, she says. When they're in front of me I can taste their dirt in the air. She touches my arm. Don't you worry about whether they deserve it or not. I know what I'm doing, I know how to make sure. Besides, she says, what does it matter? They kill us, we kill them. Fair is fair is fair.

But it's not right, that's what I'm thinking. It can't be right, can it?

WE'RE BACK AT camp when a car drives in, it's a Ford with a trailer loaded up with a tarp across it. Out of it come a woman and a man, they're taking their time. She has a white thing on her head and a blue smock, it's long-sleeved and to the ankles. Dark lace-up shoes like a man might wear, like a man in the city. Her eyebrows are shaved and her chin is round. She's following him, she's keeping a few steps behind and he's the tallest person I've ever seen. As they walk towards us I think of a cowboy. White hair and black eyebrows with a grey moustache and a collar tied at his throat. He even has a hat and as you'd imagine, it's black.

Hello there. Greetings, he says to me and that smile is something. What teeth! Queenie will say later. I'm Reverend Jones. He points to the woman and says, This is Sister. Who's in charge here?

How can we help? Queenie asks.

I look at the helpmate because I understand right away that's what she is. The woman's face is closed but not as much as she thinks, I see the movement of her eyes. Girl has disappeared, usually she does when strangers are about.

You're not one of those women, are you? the Reverend asks.

What's that? Queenie says. She holds a hand to her ear.

We've heard they're on the road. Moving from place to place, a mobile abortary you could call it.

Oh yes, Queenie says. It is us. Assassins too. Well, she's an apprentice. She points at me. I'm a killer of men in a country where God is dead. She pauses. Look at me, she says. You think I'd be doing that? She touches her back and mimes someone struggling to walk. I'm just a little old lady, she says, and laughs. We do a show here and there, we sometimes cut hair. But I know your type, she says. You're one of those temperance men, preaching against women's rights, coming in here all hot with your accusations.

We're for the rights of everyone but mostly the unborn and it's true, we're against drinking too, we're against that, the Reverend says.

Is this your woman? Queenie asks. Does she have her rights intact?

That's not your business. He's looking around now.

Queenie sits down. Please, she points and he takes a chair but the woman stands to the back.

We're stopping it. He leans forward. We're stopping all of it.

Well, you might be stopping things but what are you doing to help? Are you making anything better or merely giving talk all over the place?

We help poor children. We help good families.

And how is that working out? Later Queenie will tell me he's not helping. He's making it worse, she'll say. Him and his religion. Making everything worse.

We help the children. He stands. That's it. He's decided he's not dealing with her anymore. It always works, Queenie told me. Get a man offside and they put you away in their mind. They can't deal with being challenged by a woman so they either break her if they can, or turn away which is what he's doing now. I know what he sees. An old woman. A teenager. A dusty lot. There's no threat here, only irritation. He's dismissing her.

Who's in charge? he asks. Where are the men?

No men, Queenie says. There are no men here.

Valentina is coming across from the truck with her dressing-gown flapping and Queenie will be annoyed but Valentina has her own tactics and sometimes they help. Soon she's standing with us, she's speaking to the Reverend.

What's your business?

There's talk of people aborting babies. Do you know anything about that?

We don't, Valentina says. What did you hear?

It's a terrible thing. Immoral. I want to talk to them. Nothing more.

Of course, Valentina says. Terrible.

What's this little show you have? he says. What's this little theatre?

Valentina lists some of the acts.

But no contortionists or flexibles, Queenie adds. No sword swallowers. We don't have them. Devil's work.

Ah. It seems we agree on that. I've always found contortion disturbing.

Queenie smiles. Yes, quite, she says.

He says he's sorry to bother us. He hands Valentina a card and adds, Telephone me if you hear anything. But he doesn't leave, he stands there. He motions to me and asks, Perhaps I could have a drink of water?

Valentina says, Go on, Win, get the Reverend a drink.

I come back and he's seated again. Queenie has gone inside the truck and now it's Valentina who's talking.

Everyone's doing their best. Me, I'm a sad clown, she's saying. I'm the little guy making his way in the world but everything is against me. I keep trying, I don't give up and people like that. They see themselves in the person who hasn't clicked yet that the dice are loaded, and loaded against them. People who aren't doing well, maybe they're being pushed around by their boss, they see my guy, they realise to submit is best.

It's all you can do sometimes. Carry on being the little person in a world that is truly puzzling.

The Reverend yawns. All very interesting, he says. But I suppose we'd better be on our way, and Valentina says, Farewell, travel safe.

She wanders off across the way and lifts a props basket out of the truck.

The man tries to talk to me again but I say I have things to mend and that he can leave the cup when he's finished but he doesn't let me go.

How old are you?

I tell him.

He's surprised. He says he thought me younger.

Do you remember that age? He says this to the woman and she makes a noise like a cough. It's strange how silent she is.

I remember that age, he goes on. Nineteen went forever, it wasn't a good time for me that's for sure. He sips the water. There's a shadow on you, girl, he says to me. I want him to finish his drink and go. Luckily he thinks me too young and Queenie too old. He's watching Valentina, she has her big shoes on now and her red nose too. She's showing them that it can't be her, that he shouldn't even consider it. We're clowns for crying out loud is what she's saying to him as she puts on her red wig.

Do you have anyone else with you? the Reverend asks.

We have the engineer, she fixes the car and the truck and she cooks too. And we have Girl but she's a little kid.

Hmmm, the man says.

I hold my hand out for the cup but he takes my wrist and I feel darkness in his fingers.

He gives me the empty cup and I say, Thank you. He says, No. Thank *you*. But still he doesn't go, rather he mentions how people are very closed these days. That it's hard to know who to trust. How people can be very guarded, even when there's nothing aberrant going on. People can act as if they're doing something that they shouldn't.

I say I suppose so, but just then they arrive, that's Girl and the engineer.

Girl is entirely wild inside of her animal. She's shouting, Look, Win!

I walk backwards as she comes upon us, her metal limbs thudding and joints screeching she turns the creature, it's as big as a small car. I'm backing up and backing up and on she comes. She's inside of it, there inside the great metal cat. I see ears and a mouth even fangs, she's moving her arms and her legs stomp the pedals and the creature responds. I can't believe it works. The engineer's built a metal lion and Girl is inside of it, bringing it forward.

We'll get the baddies with this, she yells.

Behind me the man and woman are stepping backwards as well.

Watch me, Girl shouts, and how can we not? The cage lion

swings around the gravel, its clawed feet marking the ground with deep scratches, Girl inside, pedalling hard.

Then it's the elephant, the engineer high up in a seat suspended within the framework, a kind of hammock chair that swings from chains, her hands on a wheel which controls the head. At her knees are long sticks, they have knobs on the ends, and it seems they're controlling the feet and the trunk which is a structure of overlapped tiles made of wood. The whole thing is a patchwork of materials, there's denim and leather and corduroy, and through slender gaps the metal frame is visible. The tail dangles, the ears flap. It doesn't matter that you know it isn't real because it is somehow alive. How it looks moving towards us. How it feels to have it close. People will come for this, people will surely pay to see these creations. I wonder if the engineer would make me one and I find myself thinking which animal I would like to be.

The engineer is lowering her trunk and it sweeps the ground. Touch it, she yells and I feel the rough sandpaper finish. Two eyes with long lashes made from brush wire, tusks made of something else, I see bandage wrappings underneath a white coating of paint.

Go under, she yells again and I walk underneath. I stretch my arms up and touch the belly. How can it be possible to flat-pack such a thing? And how is it run? Hybrid system, the engineer will tell me later. E-traction and battery. Simple.

There's little reaction from the man and woman. What strange people they are.

You all related? The Reverend's asking the question. He says it again to me.

Sort of, I tell him.

They say they're leaving, they say goodbye and go to their car.

Valentina comes across and hands me the card.

Doctor + Physicologist, Metaphysics, Theology + Elixirs, and a phone number.

I watch the car pull out with the woman driving and as they go past she's looking right at me.

THE WOMAN

DOWN THE ROAD he says, Did you hear what she said? The child? About the baddies?

I tell him I did.

Did she mean us? he asks and I reply, Surely not.

The old one is too old, he says, and the other too young and those two in between, it's neither of them. They were unfriendly but I know how it works, how travelling people keep to themselves. Mind your own business, don't mess up someone else's game. Pay your debts before you leave the lot. I learned it with the carnivals. He stops talking and is quiet so long I think he might have gone to sleep. But then he speaks again. Those mechanics, though, he says. Impressive, don't you think? Reminded me of a Meccano set, do you know what that is?

I don't know what he's talking about, I don't know any of it. He's from another time, he's much older than me. And something's not sitting right for him. He keeps saying he knows how it works, he knows the routine, and he starts to talk about blow-offs and girlee shows. Men sneaking back in the dark, paying extra, he says. How shows would have other acts, special ones for money. Those mechanicals, what did you think? They're going to use them to make money as a side I suppose, and part of me thinks why not but part thinks it unnatural.

I keep my attention on the road. There's a granular aspect to the air, a grittiness, and I tasted it especially strong at their camp. Increasingly there is murk. It's washed over the land and I wonder if it's infected him. If it's the reason for his recent despair.

I steer the car back to the highway. My hunger is waning, it's something that visits me in waves and leaves. Sometimes I'm sure I will never eat again, and with that thought comes a small vibration of energy and I know it will be enough to carry me on a bit longer.

—

We're down the road a way and I'm thinking about them, the mechanimals, those structures of steel and fabric, as if they were come from the Earth to find me, speaking to me in language that was part foreign, part familiar. I don't have the words to describe how alien they were yet how elemental. I recognise there is a sadness within me. I can't bear to think of those machine animals. It's taken me this time to realise why it is and I suspect it's because while such automatics are impressive, in the end they are without a soul, they have no life essence. I saw the jacks and pulleys and that the large one had a motor rather than a heart, and this sadness in me has come from imagining them, as if such things might be in some way aware of their own lack of blood and skin. There is nothing natural about them. They are trying to be something they're not, they are an approximation. Ah, I have it, I know what it is. They aren't even dead. They have not had the chance of being alive. We see roadkill every day and when we do I imagine their life energy having left them, either with a violent pull or a gentle drifting of spirit strings that rise silver from the body and trail to the sky. Those creatures are gone to a better place other than beside a lonesome stretch of road but these dull structures of vinyl and tin haven't ever breathed so they can never die.

I don't think I've ever been sadder than to think about something as this.

IT'S A FAIR walk to town. Across the bridge and into the main street takes twenty minutes. The inn sits midpoint and shop windows are dirty, sprays of black thrown up by the wheels of motor cars or trucks. Likewise, the feet that tramp the unpaved paths, they toss dirt to the walls, someone should clean them. I see steps broken that no one has bothered to repair, rickety horse ties from back when people would stop awhile. Water troughs in the street, dry for most of the year of course, no one would take a hose to them now, there's no need.

We're in the street and there are people moving about, opening shops. The usual assorted goods on display, mostly tinned though some fresh fruit and bottles of water. Salvaged items from hard rubbish. I see vacuum cleaners, coffee machines, mobile phones, GPS devices. Along the street, homeless sit with their hands out. He checks his coat pocket, there are pamphlets and he gives them along with five dollars each to the line of women on the ground. Paper money, he tells them. How about that? A finger cocked with his thumb erect, a child's gun symbol and a synchronous click at the side of his mouth. He is satisfied with his generosity and walks on.

In some places it's necessary to apply lubrication, that's what he calls it, either ahead of a revival or as a salve afterwards. If townsmen become disturbed at what they hear about his speechifying, he asks them along to the next meeting and mollifies them with words or cash or a little of both, there being less cash than words these days. In the past, it was a nice dinner or an invitation to the races, and we enjoyed many such times but now his focus is narrowed. He's interested in finding the people who rip babies from the wombs of their mothers. Right now it's coffee he's after but first we have to meet with a man from the council. He holds out his pocket watch: five minutes. The coffee will have to wait.

We stop outside the inn, the man we're meeting is there. Another proud mayor, his billboards proclaim the location as one of superior rivers, greenery, fruit and culture. It's a place of wealth and opportunity, they have art exhibitions at the town hall and a big band sometimes plays in the square. We set off down the road. The mayor's talking about all of it but the Reverend isn't listening, I can tell from the angle of his head. Men like this rub at him with their incessant talking. The mayor keeps on. Now it's the floods up north, the drought down south, the fires to the west and the fishing wars to the east. After that it's the plants grown in the civic gardens, they use recycled water of course. For our benefit, he lists them off: rainwater, bore water and the tears of local citizens. He glances sideways to gauge whether this joke has been registered and is disappointed. He goes on. The fruit was traditionally pineapples but in current times it's the cherry and he tries to explain it's because the people prefer cherries, that they consider them a less aggressive fruit. But we know. We know the history of pineapples and we're tired of him. We don't want him walking alongside with his chatter. This is the type of person who needs to be filled up by the good opinions of others and we are bored by such people.

Hmmm. Tell me now. The Reverend has hold of the man's arm. What did you want to be when you were a child?

Beg pardon?

When you were little. What job.

Probably a truck driver or fireman, the man says.

The Reverend says that for him it was cowboy or astronaut. That a cowboy could ride on his horse wherever he wanted to, but a spaceman, well he was the one who could go up into the atmosphere, to the moon and other planets.

I was a child when they walked up there the first time, the Reverend says. As a boy I wanted to learn all there was to know. I found out that *Apollo* was the first spacecraft with people on board to reach the moon and go around it and return. They were the first to see an earthrise. They made a Christmas broadcast by reading from the Bible. The first American to spacewalk had a star of David and crucifix and medallion of one of the saints. He took these things with him, wanted to keep them close even when he himself was the furthest from Earth that a man had ever been. Don't you find that moving?

The government man doesn't know what to say but the Reverend doesn't notice. He continues talking.

I've always been more science-inclined myself, I studied part way to be a doctor. I didn't finish but what I gained in knowledge has been helpful, with the butchery even, you could say. Did I mention? I used to be a butcher in my younger years.

The mayor nods. Makes sense, he says. Muscles and tendons and that. He's happier now to be on a topic he can understand, I imagine the space talk was too confronting for him. He didn't like where it was leading, which might have been, perhaps, to a question about his own system of beliefs. But the Reverend doesn't realise when others aren't connecting with what he is telling them, or maybe he sees but doesn't care. These days it's as if the closer he comes to death, the less of a hold he needs to keep over himself. He talks more is what I've noticed.

Do you know how the world will end? he asks. They say it won't be with a bang, they say it will be slow, with a series of explosions, one after the other, stars stopping in bursts gradually until they evaporate. All the energy will go out of the universe, which will be like an untied balloon you let go of, it'll fizz at the end like a balloon. They're worried about this extinction event on Earth but the energy of the universe is running out.

The mayor is smiling. His mind has stopped on balloons.

I do know that about balloons, he says. I remember them from before, we had them at parties, but the rest of it? The universe? It sounds right. It's a bit sad, really. He squints and looks up.

What do you think they're talking about up there right now? the Reverend asks.

The man doesn't know. He doesn't have the capacity for more than one thought in his head at a time. The end of the world and balloons is already too much for him.

The Reverend stops and we stop as well. I see a haberdashery, a dentist. Screen printers, a hair salon. A cafe.

Now, the Reverend says. If you don't mind, I'd like some quiet so I can work on my speech. I do it up here. He taps his forehead and points at the cafe. Is this a good place for coffee?

Sure, it could well be, the man says. I don't take it myself but I've heard people say it's good. They do a nice pie.

Excellent. We wave at him and say goodbye and go in and take a seat.

The Reverend orders coffee for us both and a slice of cherry pie fresh-made for himself. The coffee is hot and good.

Ah, he says. This gives me faith that there still exists a decent brew in the world. That there's more choice for a mug of steaming than those cursed chains. This is good, isn't it?

I say that it is.

He orders a second coffee to take away and I shake my head when he gestures to me. It comes in a paper cup and the lid is cardboard too.

What a rort that was, he says. Plastics banned now. Back to paper. Invent something, sell it, then make it illegal. What was the point of it all? Send people down one avenue only to blow a whistle and call them back. No, that's the wrong way, this way, this way. Hustling and shepherding so no one notices what's going on at the end of the street. Shysters and cheapjacks, all of them.

I listen and produce my small sounds of agreement.

ANOTHER TOWN, THIS one known for a particular type of parrot that used to flourish but which no one has seen for more than a decade now, maybe two. The crowd is different here, closed. He tells me he hopes they will accept more from him, that they'll absorb one of his stronger sermons. I can only try, he says to me beforehand. What's the worst that can happen?

—

He's onstage, he begins.

Have you heard? Young girls being disfigured by their parents and older ones self-maiming so they won't draw the attention of men. What is this? Does anyone know whether this is truth or a fiction? Women ridding themselves of their pregnancies, well this is nothing new. But girls and women doing it to themselves. We are back a hundred years and I hear their methods are barbaric.

A clutch of children and toddlers sprawl in a mass in front. Infants with dribbling mouths, their slick chins catching the light, and older children with matted hair and turned eyes. The girls in the crowd, they stand further back in the tent and hunch over their pubescent bodies. They want to remain unseen but their bodies, out of their own control, have become beacons to those who wish to do them harm. They walk on the streets with their arms crossed over their developing chests, curving their backs protectively around themselves. It happens around eleven or twelve, it can be before they've even started bleeding. Someone has spoken to them, said something, maybe it was on the road, from a car, a van. They've received public comment on their body, they've received appraisal and judgement. It's made them know in that instant with a kind of violence that they are now prey. Boys are here too with tension in their own faces and bodies. To save their own selves they must become animal. I know it's not so simple. I know it, but still it is part of the whole.

He keeps talking. We can't hear you, someone calls.

Hands to mouth he shouts: Women need help but they are going about it wrong. It's all wrong.

People stamp the ground and clap.

He goes on. We're in battle now, I need you in the fight. Are you with me? This is not a time to be neutral. People who 'don't know' and people who 'aren't sure', there is no place for you here. Go find a spiked fence and throw yourself across it. Once that egg is fertilised IT IS LIFE. A thing of wonder and majesty, and it must be treasured and protected at any cost. People talk of medical emergencies and they talk of exceptions but I don't accept their exceptions. A mother is in service to her growing baby from the beginning. She must put her doubt to the side along with any mental conditions that make it challenging for her. There are people with diseases of mind and body and we must feel sad for them. They are sad. I feel sorry. Sad! Sorry! But she must put the baby first. From the point of fertilisation she is the keeper, nothing else. It is her role and, whether acknowledged or not, it's her future. Either raising healthy children or facing prison terms. They want choice, THIS IS THE CHOICE. This is what I wish for the women who kill their babies.

He does not judge or slander desperate women, he says. He does not call them whores. He sees the truth about them, that they're doing evil out of urgent need and that they must be helped. If you've heard anything you can speak to Sister.

It's time to kneel. He gets down, it takes a while. The wooden boards that form the stage are a wonky assemblage. There is a cushion and he's glad for it. His voice drops and he becomes calm. But the women who aren't desperate? he says. Those women who kill their child for convenience? Out of selfishness? Those ones? His voice is rising. They are COCKSUCKING WHORES who will burn in HELL.

OUT THE WINDOW the United Petroleums, the derelict visitor information lounges, botanic gardens and central schools. We stop for meetings along the way. Next comes a river town and we rest there a night. Then we're deep in bush at the foot of a mountain for an afternoon, and after that we're back near the river but at another bend, where it flattens out in a wide scree of light-coloured stones. A farmhouse standing alone, its roof collapsed from the weight of sand driven by wind from the drylands. Carcasses on the road, they're birds mostly, but sometimes larger beasts, bloated bodies dragged to the side. A winged vee of cranes high in the sky, their behaviour still making sense in a world where so much that was regular has abandoned us.

The trees here are all the colours of green. I've sometimes dreamed my last view will be one of landscape with a wide lens to take in the saltbush and pepperberry. I think I'll still be sat here in this car when it happens, or maybe it will be on a frozen night on my bedroll. You might say I'm too young to think of such things and perhaps you're right, but my dreams have gone to a place of dark poetry. I've always thought purpose was enough but now, oh, how long we can take to wake. I'm realising purpose not only needs to exist but that it must be correct. He wants to cleanse himself because he fears an ending in flames but for me it's another question and one that I meditate on every morning as I wake and every night as I close my eyes. The days are joined now into constant existence without pause: Why am I here? In the world?

I tell you, I do not know why.

—

The weather is shifting towards full storm and I can feel it about me, that particular smell. How the damp spreads from far away. How the night air comes to wrap around your body. There's rain now and thunder to follow I expect, and in the distance sheets of lightning in the sky. And now I'm wet, I'm coming from the river with my canvas bag and I stop and I show him: two firm catfish with good eyes.

These can be your tea if you like.

He prods one of them. Who wouldn't like? he says. The Lord provides.

And so He does, I reply.

I take the fish away, to a bucket in the rain. I'm careful of the spines as I squat and slit those bellies and pull those innards, scraping the scales onto a rock. Blood congeals on my fingers and my nails will stain red with it, with the blood, but I can't worry about that.

I hope I don't catch chill or I'll be coughing tomorrow but even so, perhaps I can manage to pack the cavities with bitter mustard greens of the type he likes. I find them growing along the banks and I chop them and mix them with lard and dried berries. My mouth becomes juicy as I think of such a dish and I hunker there in the rain and soon come the earth smells, they are so sweet to me. Citrus gum too. I stay, and stay a moment longer, listening to myself breathe.

—

He is unsettled, even his tonics are failing. I think he needs to sleep more but he says he cannot. If we had valerian drops he might but we don't. He lies down on his cot in the afternoon to reflect, he keeps his suit coat and necktie in place but his hat goes on his belly and all the world vanishes with light slumber until the dreams appear. This time there are animals. Giant and metallic like a scene from a film. At the end of his nap, before I step in to awaken him with my furtive touch, he finds himself deep in torment. After the mechanics come horned demons, and laughter. *What are you doing?* a voice shrieks at him. *What are you doing?* All of this he relates to me afterwards, there in the tent.

The light is not so lovely without the dark. We know the darkness is necessary. We're in it and it's in us and it's thick as rank stew. Unmeasurable but not unseen. I say none of this to him, of course.

Nothing new, he says. What has been will be again. What has been done will be done again. For some this might be a comfort but I see now that it is a torture for him. It hangs in the air, the idea that nothing changes, and while the act of forgetting, of excuse, makes for the continuance of life, it also makes for the perpetuation of wrong. All of this is what consumes him, what keeps him up when he should be asleep. The idea that all has been for nothing.

Another question for me these days, though, and it comes at me in the night, circling with the ferocity of a vast thing that has squeezed out from another world into ours, is this: What awaits me out there beyond this small ring of light, beyond him, beyond his work?

WIN

THERE'S NOT A person as kind as Queenie, with the women I mean. What she does is sit in a quiet way. She lets them be however they are, she lets them tell her what they choose. She calls them her girls and says it's about us being there for anyone who needs it. That this is a safe place for women and children, that she doesn't want to hear any talk of men's rights.

They've got the whole world, what do they care about our little business? Don't be a helpmate, Win, she says. Don't waste your time with them either, the helpmates I mean.

She says these sorts of things and then puts on the music. The songs are what she remembers from when she was younger. Queenie plays the whole record but the song she likes the most is about a pineapple, a gift a man gives to a woman. It pleases her this song and she sings it as she gets the instruments ready. She sings loud on certain words, they're always the same ones.

If you DIAMONDS, if you . . . PEARLS. If you . . . ROSES . . . other GIRLS. PINEAPPLE . . . ta da ta da . . . for . . . ME.

Men aren't worried about what it's like to be a woman, she says. No curiosity. They're thinking how awful it is to be a man, how everyone is against them. How things have been spoiled by women making complaints, speaking up. They think if they wait that we'll move on and talk about something else, that we'll get distracted. That we'll notice the crumbs on the bench and go to wipe them away. Well, this time we aren't getting distracted.

It's like she's a soldier and she's explaining a strategy. She's here for the reclamations, to bear witness to women's pain and do dispatches when they're needed. I don't know why she wants to do any of it because all of it is hard.

—

Other things can be broken down to help with understanding, like the big roosters, but also for acceptance, for learning where to put the line. For example, there's a blood clot or a small clump of cells or a too-small infant, it's almost full-term but it's also unwanted and it might be that the baby is alive. This is how it might be done, how it can be possible to accept. A decision, a choice, a plastic bag. Queenie says they aren't yet ensouled so it doesn't matter, or it doesn't matter as much as the woman does. That if one of them is to live it has to be the woman. If you ask me, though, as long as we live in a world where we eat animals, and humans are what has killed the Earth, do we really think we're that good? Are we that worthy of protection?

—

A woman arrives at a rest stop, appears from nowhere. She doesn't have an appointment and is asking for the hairdresser.

You have the wrong people, Queenie tells her. We're not who you want.

She sends her away, polite but definite.

She's a spy, Queenie says. It's important you know one when you see one.

How can you tell? I ask, but she can't describe it to me. All she says is, It's a feeling, Win.

You have to work it out on your own, she says, and adds that she always tries to say yes. I don't say no, not if I can help it. I said no once because the woman was too big and she killed herself the next day so my no didn't help her in the end, did it? I do everything I can to say yes. I tell women to come to me early, I tell them to come as soon as they can, but this one today, she was a spy.

That night I wonder about the spy and I wonder how I can trust my feelings. What it might feel like to know something in that way. What it would feel like to be certain.

—

When we go through towns, we pass houses that have their own music playing loudly, something I've noticed since I was little. I've worked out what it's for, it's to cover screaming. We hear people shouting in gardens or on the street and once a man chased a woman in front of us. The engineer stopped the truck and the woman fell against the bonnet. She was wearing a wedding dress and it was her face as she was pressed there, it was her face we all saw. She was crying, he was behind her, and it's her eyes I can't forget. We watched as the man pulled her, he carried her off the road. He put her in his car and he took her away.

THEY TOOK AWAY the blind musicians, there were three hundred of them. Stalin made them get on trains to go to a special meeting, they said it was some sort of conference. First it was the bandoleers and the lyre players but then they got around to the hurdy-gurdists. It's not clear when it was, the 1920s or '30s, but they shot them. They took them into a forest and shot them and burned their instruments. People like to think it was because they didn't like the sound of the music but Valentina says it's because they didn't like what the songs said to people, what those national ballads told of the old freedoms. However people felt, Stalin said that life was better now, that life was merrier. He had it printed on posters and flyers and the people believed him because they didn't have a choice.

—

Hurdy-gurdies were played by blind men who wandered the countryside to be with families and pray for their loved ones who'd died. They stood outside village houses and played and they stood in doorways in St Petersburg to sing their epic laments of the enslaved, of the lost and of the newly dead.

First comes the drone. You turn the handle, like I've said already, round and round it goes, and it's the hum that hypnotises you. It's the drone that doesn't stop for the whole of the song and then the one after. It's the drone that brings the feelings, like the bagpipe. Valentina says it's the drone that is life, she says it's a kind of breath. To me it feels like hope. It keeps going and going and it keeps going some more until it stops. Maybe that's when you die. When the drone stops.

—

Valentina says there are two types of people, that's children and philosophers but three types of clown, which is Tramp or Whiteface or Auguste. Most people think of themselves as Whitefaces, they think that's best because they want to be the boss, they want to be in charge. Valentina says Bugs Bunny was a Whiteface but I don't know who that is. Whitefaces are the ones who throw the pies, they don't take the hit. No one wants to be an Auguste but Valentina says they're the best of all. It's the Auguste who has heart and they're the one who will break yours. They try to cope with life but it's not a fair fight. They're the one who keeps loving a person even when the other person might have stopped. They're the person who keeps smiling when someone is being cruel. They bring a gift to someone who has never once been kind. It's the Auguste who is tender-hearted, the one who stays gentle and good no matter what. The Whiteface might dominate that's true, and it might be them who triumphs and who has the power but what is that sort of winning when a heart is cold? Who cares about having the gold if no one loves you, if no one even likes you? What's the good of that?

—

Valentina says Stalin was a Whiteface and that Khrushchev was an Auguste but I don't really know about that. What I do know is that Queenie is a Whiteface. She was hurt by a husband and it made her sad and hard. Even though she tries her best, she's a Whiteface all the way through.

—

It's important to understand what makes people laugh because then you can be deliberate, you can have intention. Profanation is important in clowning which is simple, it's about things being wrong. Wrong place, wrong person, wrong time, wrong size. It's funny to have something in the wrong place, like a dog as a hat.

You can have the wrong people in the right place, like a baby dressed up as a businessman. Things of the wrong size can be funniest of all or doing something when you shouldn't or not doing it when you should, it's that kind of thing. Imagining it can make you smile, can't it? A clown with a tiny hat on her head, that's funny isn't it? Or a banana strapped to her wrist instead of a watch. Think about it if you have a spare moment. Even prisoners can smile, in the dark if they have to.

Things being used wrong is funny and Girl's good at it. We have an act where I give her instructions and she misunderstands and does them all wrong, like: Put this apple over there on the table and she puts it on her knee, that's wrong place. You do it wrong but your face shows you think it's right. This is how easy it is. A person catching a ball and they put their hands up after the ball has already hit them on the shoulder, wrong time. A tiny violin in a big case, a big person in a tiny car, you get the idea.

It's the Auguste who's always wrong, that's why they're the best. They're the most popular type of clown, so popular it's enough to make the Whiteface want to smash them in the nose with a ribbon.

—

We're the clowns. The three of us are Zippo and Bobo and Gigi. Girl's character is Zippo, she's the Whiteface, that's it that's all. I'm not even sure if it's female or male or somebody else but none of that matters, it's what the Whiteface does that's important. A Whiteface is easy to create. It's easy to play mean, they never soften and especially not when others are upset. When someone else is crying it makes them meaner. They take over the stage and they're loud and frenetic and Girl likes this. She loves to stomp around the ring with big steps being noisy, letting her body go extreme. Valentina told me it would be good for her confidence so that's why she made Girl the Whiteface. Whitefaces put out a lot of energy and noise so it seems they're doing more than they really are. They're the ones to take over the action, they're the ones who force others to listen. Because Girl's the Whiteface, Valentina told her she's the smartest of the troupe and that made her do a handstand, Girl that is.

I'm Bobo, the Tramp, the one who bends down to pick up a flower while the pie misses and goes into the face of the Auguste, which is Gigi, that's Valentina. While the Tramp sometimes gets it over the Whiteface, the Auguste never does. An Auguste is the loser of any group they're in but like I said before, the Auguste is the one everyone loves. The Auguste rushes into the ring, running late or running early, never on time, and no matter how they try, they can't get it right. They fall over everything, it can be their own feet, a broom leaning nearby, objects big and small, and they do it all wrong, even the simplest of things. When they try to put an arm into their coat it goes into the lining and it's this that makes the audience laugh, it's this that causes the heart to be happier in that moment than it ever has been. The Auguste makes you love them but they aren't even trying. We watch an Auguste and can know all the ways our lives aren't successful and for some of us it means we can say life is mostly beautiful instead of mostly terrible. Augustes bear everything that gets thrown at them and Valentina says we should all try to be this type of clown as much as we can in our real lives. That we should all try.

—

Valentina showed Girl how to use a burned cork to draw a moustache. She showed her how she does it, under her nose. You could call it a Chaplin but we all know the other name for it. Valentina says there's a connection between poetry and clowning, she says both are to do with acrobatics but that there's philosophy too which can help us figure out the world around us. The press of a wrist, the scrape of a shoe, a few words spoken from a stage. It's the perfect compact image which can say so much. Afterwards, there's the shock of understanding. You leave the show, you turn the page. You close your eyes. You have been transformed.

IT TURNS OUT I can't do the dispatch. Queenie gives me her straight razor, she calls it a cutthroat. We're in the truck and in front of us the man is sitting in the special chair. It tips back so we can get the towel on him, the face towel made hot and wet from the bowl. He groans when she puts it on and there's something off about that sound, something to do with sex. Queenie looks at me as if to say, See!

She wraps it around him, the towel that is. It's covering all of his face, it's across his eyes and chin with his nose sticking out and a gap underneath where his neck shows, open and white.

She says, Two minutes for the pores, and she and I stand behind him. She passes me the razor, she pushes it into my hand. Tilts her head at him.

I've never seen her slice one because she said I couldn't just watch, that it would make me scared, that I had to do one myself. Press harder than you think you need to, is the other thing she said.

But I am scared, I am, and I can't do it. She takes the razor from me and points to the door. I go outside. I wait on a fallen tree and not long after she comes out, she has blood on her gloves. She calls the engineer who walks from around the back. She goes inside, she shuts the door behind her so she can do the next part. Queenie walks over to me. She asks what's wrong with me.

What's wrong with you, Win? That's what she says. What's wrong with you?

—

Later the engineer takes the man in bits to Pet. That's where they go, into our tiger. Queenie says they don't deserve such an ending after what they've done. For these men to be eaten by a tiger, she says, it's too noble if you ask me. But what else can we do? We can't bury them, she says.

It's disgusting and I don't blame you if you think it's wrong, I don't blame you if it makes you hate us. Perhaps it is wrong, probably it is, but like Queenie says what else can we do? The time for talk is over. No more talk. It's enough.

I'M YOUNGER AND carrying a bag of potatoes, this is at Arcadia when Pearl was still with us. A woman comes out of the trailer, her hair is done and she's crying. I tell her it looks nice but she pushes past me. It's not about hair, she says and gets into her car and drives away. I go through the annexe to the trailer. I open the door and step in without knocking, which is the exact thing I'd been told never to do. First I hear the music, it's the pineapple song that I told you about before.

In the kitchenette is Pearl, she's near the sink, she's standing with a bundle of newspaper in her hands, it's wrapped up like a parcel. When she sees me she makes a noise and the paper slips, it comes open. Out falls something, it could be a fish but it has legs and arms just starting. It's grey with blood and eyes that are closed and black.

Is it a bird? I ask and we both look at it on the floor.

Queenie pushes open the concertina door at the end with her knee. There's a little sleeping area and I see the feet of someone, it's another woman she's lying flat on the bed.

What happened? Queenie says to Pearl and then she notices me.

I look at what she has in her hand and it isn't scissors or a comb. I look at her other hand which is gloved and red. Her shoes have funny covers.

What are you doing in there? I ask.

Get her out. Queenie's voice is very cold.

She came in, I didn't hear her. Pearl is hunched over the mess on the floor, she's starting to wrap it.

What is that? I'm still standing in the doorway.

Queenie says, You deal with it, and goes back inside the little room. I hear low voices. I hear the woman saying, Alright.

Why does Queenie have that mask? I ask. Is it a perm?

Pearl doesn't say anything.

It's not hairdressing is it, I say and she says, No, it's not.

She tells me to sit down, that she has something I need to hear and it's that they don't cut hair or set curls. Well, we do, she says, but not always. We help them with a problem. We make it go away.

Is that a baby?

No, it isn't, it's not a baby, it's only the beginnings.

Is that what you're doing? You're taking them out?

Pearl tells me to boil the kettle but I don't move.

We have to keep things clean, she says. She gets down on her knees, she's wiping the floor. Things will smell if I don't do this properly.

I sit and watch as she cleans up. She uses disinfectant and when she finishes she says, That's better.

I'm still sitting there when Queenie comes out, she's holding the woman by the elbow. The woman has curlers in her hair and is walking very slowly. Queenie takes her down the steps to the annexe then Pearl goes down too and settles the woman on the couch. She asks if she would prefer tea or coffee and I hear no, just water please, she says she's very thirsty so Pearl gets that and a biscuit. She holds the jar out to me but I shake my head. I don't want a biscuit. Pearl says, Suit yourself, and goes to hang the cloth.

I see it drying outside when I leave.

—

Queenie's asking me a question and Pearl's there too.

I'm not sure, I say.

Queenie's at the window.

I can keep going a while longer, Pearl says.

That's when I realise that Pearl wants to stop. She wants to finish up, she's tired of the travel.

Queenie comes over to me. She puts her hands on my cheeks, I know what she's doing she's trying to be persuasive. She tells me fourteen is old enough. Old enough to learn about the steriliser and the gas, they use it in a vaporiser. To know that it's about saving women's lives. She makes it all sound simple and I can see how important it is to her. She says, You don't need to think, just do it for old Queenie, won't you? She looks like she does when she's being ringmaster, when she goes all unnatural because being charming isn't something that's easy for her. It makes me feel uncomfortable so I say yes to stop that feeling. I guess that's why it works, her manipulation I mean.

Now she holds my shoulders.

It's because I'm worried you might need one and that I won't be here to do it for you, she says. I can teach you then you can pass it on.

I say okay, that I'll help her, because if I don't she'll get upset. It wasn't until recently that I realised what she said didn't make sense, about me needing one someday. But then it was too late.

—

After Pearl leaves, after she packs up and says goodbye to all of us, that's when Queenie says she can't trust Pearl anymore.

But I can trust you, can't I? she says to me. You'll be alright, you'll get on well enough.

I didn't know what she meant then and I'm still not sure but to tell you the truth I don't think I am, I don't think I am getting on well but Queenie needs help and I'm the only one who can do it.

Queenie's too old to care about the world much anymore. Her body aches and sometimes she needs me to rub her legs, I've done it since I was small. Sometimes in the evening after dinner before we go to bed, I rub her legs and Valentina ends by saying, Let's go round the table and everybody say their dreams. I say I don't have any and Girl tells us she can't decide there are too many. And I don't want to say the bad ones, she says. The engineer is quiet, she never talks much and Queenie says it's time for bed because dreams are for the old days, they have no place here.

—

She's cold about the past. It's not very often you can get her to admit what she misses but when she does, first it's the smell and next it's the elephants. It's the smell from the waste, the ammonia. She says it made for bad headaches but that she misses it all the same. How the smell of dung would mix with wildflowers and hay and how lovely it was to have all of that coming through the caravan's flywire screen of a summer afternoon. That's what she says, and when I ask her what ammonia smells like she says chemical and sharp and I can't see how that would be a good smell, how she could miss that at all.

—

We're at the fire, it's night-time again and Queenie is talking. Mr Gold—that's my father-in-law, may he rest in peace—he was the best tent-maker in the country. My Frank and Pearl, they sat sewing the new one by lamplight and through all the hot days while the rest of them waited in the shade. It took them four weeks to finish that tent and everyone was getting toey by then. The fabric was Scotch sail canvas, it was the best, you can't even find it today. It cost two shillings per yard, that was dear back then. It had a very tight weave, it didn't need waterproofing and it took that long 'cause it was that bloody big, excuse my. Everything had to be stitched at least double, and triple in places, and on top of the stitching was the webbing so you add that in and you've got forty feet of canvas that has to be run up and down the sewing machine, and as the pieces got joined together it became harder, you can imagine all that fabric, it was stiff as and always underfoot, so we started to help by pulling it out and trying to get it as straight as possible. Pearl worked the machine, she was the only one who could manage it, and she kept swearing each time the cotton snapped. It broke thousands of times and the canvas got all dirty from the ground, small sticks and burrs oh you can imagine, it was a blasted nightmare.

But this is how show families are, she says. They pull together strong like you wouldn't believe. Show families are triple-stitched but believe me that tent was hard. My head was throbbing from the heat and my wrists and arms aching from trying to spread the pieces of fabric out flat, so Lord knows how Pearl suffered. But we got it done and then you should have seen her face. Walking around it, touching it as if it were some holy relic. Pulling off a little bit of extra cotton here. Pinching it between her fingers and grinning, sticking her tongue out at me. She was a terrific bird. She wore those old-fashioned black cashmere performance tights, she darned them constantly. Yes, she was a bloody terrific bird, excuse my. We tumbled together and did the acrobat shows, they called us the Golden Girls, they even had it on the sign. The Golden Girls. That was us.

So everyone was happy with the tent, and Pearl and Mr Gold and Frank they were all happy too. They stood and watched it go up. Usually they had jobs elsewhere and it was only the hands who worked on getting the tent done but because it was the new one, well of course everyone was there. They pounded the pegs and there was coils and blocks everywhere. People yelling at the kids to keep back, that was the town children. They always appeared, it was like they could smell us coming, like rain you could say.

The king poles, we got them done quick, then the men got all the sections of canvas and Mr Gold he dressed the poles, he was that particular, everything was done proper because if things weren't locked in correct there'd be no way to get the trapeze or lights done and we'd be in trouble then or, even worse, it could come down during a show. You'd think the worst thing might be the cats getting out or the clowns drowning or even a fire but the worst of all is a tent coming down.

After everything had been finally checked, he made the signal, that's Mr Gold, and one of the elephants it was probably Cleopatra, she walked forward and raised it up and then after that it was easy to get it finished. Then it was seats and lights, and we laid out the ring, we gave it a good sawdusting and after that, while the hands ate lunch and had a nap, the rest of us did our practice.

That tent was a monster, Queenie says, and it stood up to all storms that came our way. But the other thing that came our way was pretty much the end. I know what Queenie's going to say and she does: Television. It took a few years to get into homes and everyone was glad that Mr Gold was gone by then because if he hadn't of been in the ground already it would of killed him for certain.

Who's Pearl? Girl asked.

She was Frank's sister. She was a good friend, Queenie goes on, and a good sister-in-law. It was hard when I first joined but she made it easier. Yes, she was a good friend. When we were younger we used to go to carnivals, we knew people at all of them and it was the Tilt-a-Whirl what Pearl loved the most. I couldn't ever enjoy it. I tried it once but it was too unpredictable for me. You'd think you knew how it was going to go and first it was going this way and then suddenly it would jerk back but not completely change direction, then it would change again and you'd carry on in the first direction, but not for long because it would change once more. You couldn't get a handle on how it was going and it did my head in, I'll tell you that straight. But Pearl loved it, she said you had to give yourself over to it. To just let go. I can see her now, laughing with her head rolling which was fine for her but not for me. I found regularity with my Frank, he was easy to love. No chaos in the man but that ride was too much for me. She would go on it over and over if we let her, laughing hysterically the whole while.

Girl has moved closer. She leans against me and listens to Queenie.

It sounds fun, she says.

I didn't think so, Queenie says. Making you believe it was a nice ride going along slowly and then speeding up, I didn't mind that part. It was the changing direction I hated, I'm saying it straight. I can still remember how it was, like being thrown around by something much stronger than you.

Like when the clown throws me high in our acrobatics?

No, it was different to that. That's just one way, up and then the other way is down. This wasn't like that. I couldn't wait to get off and never went on again.

—

Once I asked Queenie if loving Frank fixed anything for her.

At first she didn't understand what I meant. Do you mean the horseraces when he'd take the elephants across? I know what she's talking about, how he'd stand them at the bend to get the horses to act up and bookies would pay him. I shake my head. Oh, you mean our van? He fixed that up real nice. And he got me the piano, you've heard about that too. He had Cleo pull it on a dray, you should have seen it.

I say no, not that.

Oh, she said after thinking a bit. You mean made me think that men could be alright? No, love. It doesn't work like that. He was one man. He understood me and he saw why I needed to do the reclamations. It was something I didn't have to explain. He told me to do what I felt was right.

Then after a few moments more she said, Oh. You're wondering about love? If all of it can be fixed with love?

I didn't say anything. I could see she was trying to be kind but even so she couldn't help laughing.

Win, she said, you've got a bit to bloody learn, excuse my.

ON THE ROAD are the signs, of course the usual that tell us where to go, how fast or how slow, and there's black-and-yellow ones that show the dips and curves, they tell us how the road itself will change. There's others that mention motor inns and council chambers and saddlers but now we're turning off and we're slowing down, we have to 'cause the road is gravel and that's when the other signs start. They're the ones hanging near camps, COME JOIN US AND BE ONE. It's always the same phone number, it's the one for the Saviours, but believe me that's not something we'd ever do, ring it that is. We hate the Saviours and they'd hate us too if they knew what we were doing.

Queenie said the Saviours talk about freedom but what they preach is the opposite. She said it's a cult and then Girl asked, What does that mean? and Queenie started to explain and Girl's face closed right up, she said she didn't want to hear any more. She went and sat right down the back of the truck by the porthole. She didn't talk for thirty minutes or more, not even once about pineapple or elephants or somersaults, not even once.

—

It's important to see things in the world around us and to recognise there are beautiful moments. That's what Valentina says. She thinks we can slow time that way and she encourages me to notice the colours and the sounds and smells. Once, a little while back, when she could tell I wasn't really listening, she asked What's important to you, Miss Winnstay? and all I could say was I don't know.

I ASKED VALENTINA how the ideas for the clown bits came to her, how did she think of them, and she said they didn't come from anywhere that they just are. Like jokes, you can't really know their heritage. They can't be traced which means you can't arrest the author and you can't raid a house to seize a joke or shoot it or put it in prison. A joke is compact and it doesn't require being written down. They can easily spread. The KGB did an experiment and found it took an average of six hours for an *anekdot* to travel from one end of Moscow to the other all by word of mouth. Six hours.

—

A member of the Communist Youth watches an aged peasant working with his old horse and plough, tilling the field. 'I can see it works in practice,' he says, 'but does it work in theory?' (9 hours)

—

A Russian rabbit flees to Poland and meets a Polish hare. 'Why are you running?' asks the hare.

'Stalin has ordered the arrest of all elephants.'

'But you are not an elephant,' the Pole points out, 'you're a rabbit.'

'I know,' the rabbit replies, 'but I can't prove it!' (5.5 hours)

—

What's not a joke is you can't take tissue from a corpse unless that person gave clear permission when they were alive. You can't take organs or eye parts, nothing like that. The people who want to ban abortion at six weeks, they say a non-viable foetus has more rights than the person whose body it's in. They're saying that women deserve even fewer rights than dead people.

Think about that.

VALENTINA TOLD ME about the matchbox: You have to imagine this. A clown is sweeping and decides to stop to take a break. She gets a packet from her pocket and shakes out a cigarette but it falls to the ground so she bends over to get it and sticks it in her mouth and more cigarettes fall out and then, as she bends down to pick them up, even more fall out. The broom she's holding drops to the floor too, so she throws the cigarettes into a pile of rubbish and sweeps them up. Then she pauses to light the cigarette in her mouth. She searches for her light takes out the matches opens the box but it's upside down so the matches fall to the ground. She bends to pick up a match but her coat snags on the broom handle and she can't reach. She unhooks herself and gets a match but it doesn't light. She tries a second match and this makes the box fly out of her hands onto the floor. She bends to pick it up but accidentally kicks it away. She puts the cigarette behind one ear and after kicking the matchbox a few more times, she stomps on it, is it a mouse now? A spider? She stomps to stop it moving away. Gets the matchbox, lights the match then puts it to her mouth but the cigarette's not there. With one hand she searches in her hair for it, she checks under her chin and behind her ears and meanwhile the match burns down to her fingers and she drops it. No match, no lighted cigarette. She sighs and returns to sweeping but the broom comes off the handle so now there's the bending and kicking of that as well as her hat which has now fallen off her head and is also on the floor, which is good which is deliberate because now we have three objects misbehaving at the same time and it makes it funnier than two. She only has two hands so with three things there can then be a rotation of falls: hat, broom head and broom handle. The hat ends up on the broom handle but she can't reach it so balances the stick on her forehead with the hat on top then knocks the stick away and the hat falls onto her head. To finish there are problems with sticking the broom head onto the handle which is achieved by licking the end of the handle to get it to stick but all of it fails and eventually she picks up the litter by hand and puts it into the bin.

You can build a whole performance around this.

You can build a lifetime of bits out of this one simple and pure structure.

—

Valentina is not one of the clowns who relies on slapstick. There's no honker, no blart noise behind another clown to cause them to jump or fall, she's never been one of those clowns. I guess you could say she's serious about her art. She's not for children firstly although they laugh, they laugh at anything she does, but she aims for the adults. She wants to bring them to her way of thinking and reckons she can do it with laughter. But not cheap laughs, that's for people who don't want to chew the meat. Valentina is a clown for people who want to think and feel. Clowning is not a red nose is what she says. It's a free head. If you saw Valentina in her costume you'd say, She's just a clown, what does she know? But she knows a lot. Probably the one person who knows more than her is Queenie and I only think that because when I asked Valentina where *she* learned everything she said it was Queenie, that she was the one who taught it all to her. Not about clowning but the rest of it.

She has more than eighty scenes written down. I've learned fifteen or so but she said she'll teach them all to me, of course it will take time. What a clown can do is make a person see things about themselves that they mightn't otherwise. I mean if they hadn't come to a show and seen us do *Man Hates Job* or *Mother Cries in Kitchen* or *Two Friends Fight* they might not think about their own lives. But after the show, those people will realise they're spending their lives in a way that they don't like and that they can change. They'll see that they don't need to be in an office with no window in a city or that they don't need to love a person who doesn't love them back or let themselves be treated badly by a friend. When people see truths about themselves in this way, for some it might make them laugh and for others it might make them cry but they will be feeling which is the best thing of all. If you ask Valentina, that's what she says. Even if it hurts it's always better to feel. And after realising it they might make things different for themselves or for someone else, make things better. As Valentina says, they can get up and take another tilt at the world because that's what it's about. You go on.

—

When we clown we don't go for the easy laughter that comes from oppressing others or putting someone down because that laughter isn't joyful. That's the sort of laughter that makes you small. You feel mean afterwards and the other person feels bad. When a bigger person is encouraged to laugh at a smaller person of course it's tainted. Even if you hate the other person and they're being crushed, still you shouldn't laugh because then it makes you cruel on top of dominant. Just stop. There are better things to do with your time. Move on, we clowns say.

But you have to be smart. You can't be open about everything you want to say. In 1959 the Soviet premier held the First National Meeting on Clown Craft. He criticised circus for lacking satire but one clown asked, Who will be the subject of our parody? The government is marvellous, he said, and so that's how they ended up mocking low-tier bureaucracy and incompetent doctors with state approval. Valentina says it wasn't fair, she said it's not good to be spitting down on office employees and healthcare workers, they're the people trying to help, but the clowns had no choice. They didn't have the power to make their spittle reach the eyes of the people who deserved it which was the government, the tyrants. Nobody spits in the eyes of the oppressors, not really. They didn't trust the government, they remembered that two hundred thousand people had spent time in the gulag for telling jokes. They remembered Stalin enjoyed his émigré comedy records and even liked *anekdoty,* but that didn't stop him finding some jokes very unfunny which is when people disappeared.

With the trapeze, the audience member is thinking: How can they do it? It's incredible. But with the clowns the thought is: Look. They're just like me, they're on my side. There's joy in this and there's relief too because people feel they're not alone. That's what people want. It's how they want to feel. I am not alone.

—

A rich American businessman visiting Moscow asks a sentry-man what he is doing on the walls of the Kremlin. 'I have very keen eyesight,' he says. 'I'm paid to keep watch on the horizon for the dawning of the Communist utopia.'

'Impressive,' replies the American. 'I'll quadruple your pay if you come work for me at the top of the Empire State Building and keep watch for the next financial collapse.'

'No, thanks,' says the simple Russian. 'Why give up a permanent job for a temporary one?' (2 days)

THE WOMAN

IT'S EARLY MORNING and there's a cool aspect to the day. I'm at the river and across the way the trees are silver, their leaves spinning like discs in the breeze. I write some words then tuck my notebook in my robe. My notebook, it's a small thing but thick with many pages.

I wash. It's important to attend to the neck as it's been an especially grimed journey. We follow the roads as we visit the backblocks at the edges of the towns, and it's the secondaries and even smaller tertiaries that raise the dust. There are days I can feel it in my mouth, how it grits against my teeth. Nobody knows where it's from though scientists believe there was an explosion in space and the dust has drifted to Earth, entered our atmosphere and come to rest in our world. I wonder if it's anything to do with the trips the people have been making, if it's anything to do with the people up there now. They say they're going to die.

I wipe my face and the water is clean and cold. Across the river the trees are dense and I imagine—well, I know—how the leaf litter is traditional home to the arthropods. Around me the air is filled with diptera, flocks of speck-like insects in a hanging mist of tiny bodies. Wild banks, a splash of yellow weed—it's a weed, certainly, but abundant and pretty to the eye. *Hardenbergia*? I remember a story of a man becoming entangled in the vine. That he fell and found something valuable. It wouldn't happen often like that, a fall and then a gain. But I have heard it said that in the quieter moments of entrapment we can find our path to freedom, that we can sometimes find our destiny. It's important to look around, to open your eyes, because when you do that's when you see there is beauty, there is always beauty. His fits and tempers happen on occasion but splendour is here to be noticed even in the annelids, the beetles, the spiders. I pull out my notebook and pencil again.

After a small while I feel light-headed. I should eat more but I enjoy the reach of hunger and the sharp energy and thinking that comes with it.

—

I return to camp and begin to prepare the meal. I do my tasks slowly. I used to talk a lot at the beginning but he cured me of that tendency—of that female display, is how he referred to it. He said he would rid me of my bad habits, that I was young and he would learn me, no matter how long it took. And so it came to be. The half-words caught before they exit my mouth so that now, here we are, with the silence he prefers.

This is how he wants it every morning, and myself now as well. He takes in the new day while I cook breakfast and I can feel him listening. He angles his head in a way that is pointed in its communication. You need to remember that I always notice, he said to me once.

Now, the smell of bacon. A single egg for him, more than that is wasteful, but he will eat only a portion of it. My mind becomes gentled as he bends over his plate.

When he finishes, I go to kneel in front of him on the mat. I wait until he clears his throat, sometimes it's minutes before the release is given, the sign that I can rise. But it's never a dialogue more complex than Might I go and tidy the tent? or Shall I make the car ready?

—

I pack and we leave. In this section of the great inland, above Dubbo and below Moree, we pass panel beaters, funeral parlours, turf clubs, state forests. The highway has three digits and runs north and south. We're headed south—because why not, was the reasoning. We conduct our usual business. His tonic stall, the pamphlets, the meetings he is invited to speak at.

We stop at base hospitals and caravan parks, even boarding kennels and catteries. I carry in to these places our printed sheets that tell of the next gatherings, he trusts me with this now. Long hours in a motor vehicle is punishing for both of us but as we cross another bridge there's a lift in his spirits. Arm flex and shoulder roll, he cracks his neck.

Something is coming and I want to be ready, he tells me.

I say yes. I've found it's important to be encouraging and positive. That was one of the earliest lessons. My recent slip, I do not know where that came from.

WIN

We're at Whiteacre for the show. We like the Interior Lowlands, the roads are good around here. We visit each year to perform and today we park near a hill and in the fields there are wildflowers, they're small, white and purple. I notice them when I get out of the truck.

It's practice now and Girl is standing on the wire tied off between two of the tent guy ropes. Her tummy is rounded and her back arched, and even though I put her hair in pigtails this morning it's falling out, it never stays put. The wire is low to the ground, she walks up and down and pretends to wobble and then rights herself. That's part of the act, it's when you make it seem you're about to fall. It makes it more exciting for the audience. I learned it when I was little and I taught her how to do it, she calls it a good trick. It's important she gets solid so that if I ever leave she'll be okay. Maybe one day she'll manage the double-back off a teeterboard with full twist in the first and a plain back in the second and if she could do that she would be golden. She could earn a good living and people would take care to preserve a body that can perform such a trick. Maybe then she'd have a statue of her own in one of the capital cities with flowers left for her. In the meantime I wish we had bears or a proper horse for her or the dog she really wants but we don't. We have to make the best of what we do have, that's what everyone says, mostly Queenie of course.

Girl gets down from the wire.

Was it good? she asks.

Yes, it was. The clown'll want you to start practising with a blindfold soon, I say.

What's that?

With your eyes covered by material. We tie it around your head.

I don't want to do that, Win. I don't.

I say it's okay. I say not to worry and eventually she calms.

Let's eat some bread, I tell her, so we do. It's with salted butter and delicious.

—

When it's time for the set-up, I drag the pieces of barrel out. It's smart, the engineer made it with hinges that collapse the walls down and there's the hose and the ladder, all of it in parts. I pull it out piece by piece. I haul the barrel away from the truck to the other side of the trees where the engineer is laying out the ring rope. I click the barrel pieces into each other and then the rubber lining latches to the walls. It takes a while but once it's done it's deeper and wider than you might think. From where the audience sits, it looks smaller. It's clever, I said to the engineer when she first showed me. You're really clever.

Before I open the tap, I look up and see overhead at the back of the haze how the light is starting to drop. I'd say we have plenty of time to finish but you never know how the day will run out, especially during afternoon set-up. At the truck, the hose is connected to the tank and I pull the lever and water rushes along, it begins to empty into the barrel, and before anybody pipes up let me say we recycle the water, it's usually river water too. Next is the steps, that's the ladder which will be hidden by a drop sheet. The high dive is the finale so we don't want people to see until it's time.

I call out for the engineer to help at the end. She holds the base as the ladder extends and I go up into the sky, pushing each section in front of me. Right at the top, the ladder sways but it's strong and I'm safe. Down below the engineer has it locked into the base and I practise swinging out to check the flex. It curves as I lunge, the view is good up here with the land spread below. This could be an act on its own, I think, just this. Me hanging and sweeping across the sky. I bend my leg out and extend my arm in a posh ballet move. I can see the town in the distance and the line of trees that shows where the river is. There are still lots of rivers around here and while rivers are good and mean that there are people in the area, even so there won't be many tonight. It's never a big crowd here not in Whiteacre, no offence.

I climb down to start putting the railing up for the curtain. It's long and red with gold fringing on it not a split curtain like you might be thinking, it's a simple one that we raise and drop at the right time. It's held by scaffolding ropes and another pulley system and we're proud of it, the curtain that is. It took me and Girl ages to make, it was really hard.

I call out to the engineer again. She's over at the engine now, it powers our lights, she's fiddling with the bulbs and wires, it's a hundred and ten vee. It's an old Dodge engine and sometimes flickers but it's good enough. I ask her if everything is under control and she says, Yes boss, without turning around and I say, Excellent. I like the engineer even though she's quiet and has scars on her body, pale lines that show white against her skin. When Girl first saw those scars she asked what happened and the engineer said she got distracted and that means it was the lions. You might think diving from eighty feet high is dangerous but the lions and elephants were the most risky and all trainers were killed if they went on long enough, so she must've stopped at the right time. With the dive into the pool, I like it because it's controlled. It doesn't move if you blink, it's all up to me.

Like I said, the audience is seated so they can't see when I hit the water. We fill the tank right up so that when I go in the waves splash over the edge, it's more dramatic. The ladder is wooden not metal and the barrel is lightwood, it's not heavy but it is strong. On the outside is an illustration and words. A girl with a fish tail, that's me and the writing says: HIGH DIVE MERMAID, DEATH-DEFYING + AWESOME and that's meant to be me too.

THEY SAY IT's the light that makes people feel a certain way, not what actually happens in the show. That it's the atmosphere. How the white flare flattens in the dark, how it reveals different things to different people and what might be fearsome to one is beautiful to another. It's the lighting that uncovers everything that's there but more than that it creates newness out of nothing much. What is real in the ring, what is moving there, which is us in costumes and our pony Maude with her feathers and Girl on her stilts, becomes exaggerated and made extreme and something new is formed. I can't explain it very well. Our bodies are made larger, our movements bigger than what they really are because of those black shadows. They're extensions of something real but not real themselves, shapes thrown into the darkness. Depending on where the light source is set up, some things cast small shadows and others large, it depends on where you're standing and how open your eyes are. All of this is simple, all of it basic.

—

It's almost time. Girl has set up the pathway with candles that form a line and show the audience where to go. It's full night now and we start in fifteen minutes. The engineer finishes putting up light bulbs along the sides of the dive tower and there are some in a tree nearby as well. The big spot is mounted on top of the truck which is parked in front of the ring.

The engineer is dressing a magpie goose on a paper tray. She puts oil on it and stuffs it with herbs and we'll sell it at the interval. Sometimes we have things like that and other times it might be decorated toilet roll holders or a Victoria sponge or pickled wild veg, or a little picture to hang on a wall but tonight it's the bird and lolly bags, that's all we've got.

The audience will enter from the side and find somewhere to sit, they can choose. It's flip seating, the type you find cheap and we've set them around the ring, there are maybe twenty chairs. We have additional on top of the truck in the storage but we haven't needed more than twenty for years now, things are that bad.

Queenie says crowds used to be eight hundred or even a thousand.

It's because we don't have any animals, is what Girl says.

Come and get your tights on, I tell her. Girl always wants to leave it until as late as possible to put them on. She hates them, she says the seams bother her and that she just wants to be free.

—

Queenie arrives in her suit. She plays the ringmaster and her cheeks are rouged pink. She takes her place at the box office, it's next to the truck but it's only a cardboard stand. People begin to arrive. First there's a family with two children and the kids' faces are scared, probably because it's night-time and we're out of town. Then it's a young couple and after that another young couple, maybe they're on dates. I watch them, they're holding hands and smiling. Next it's another group, this time two parents with five children, they must have bought a family ticket. A single person arrives it's a boy, it's a man, I'll call him a guy, he's in his early twenties maybe. He's on a bicycle and when he asks me where he should leave it, I can't say any words so Girl points to a tree and says, Put it over there. He does and comes back and asks me where to buy a ticket and Girl points again and says, Over there, see the lady with the hat? He walks away towards Queenie and Girl turns to me and asks, Win, what's wrong with you?

We begin. Girl and I start with our hurdy-gurdies, it's 'God Save the King' and then 'Hail Thee Well Met' and Girl's face, well it's her usual expression, blank with trying to not show how much she hates the noise but also with concentration. After that we go to our spots. We do the parade and first it's Queenie with her cane, she's walking slowly in front, and she leads our Maude who has her feathers on and leg bands too but there's no saddle because it's a bareback act, which is me. Next it's the engineer and her costume is red pants and a silver top and she's juggling as she goes. Then it's Girl and me and Valentina following, we're in our Wild West outfits. Queenie says we might be the smallest show on Earth but we try to do the biggest things.

Tell others about Gold's Family Show, Queenie is saying to the audience. She's talking loud so everyone can hear. Tell them that even though the art of show and clown is dying, maybe even dead, we are here and we are now, and will do our best to give you everything what we have in our hearts.

The audience claps and it all seems fine but she said 'dead' and one of the children starts crying so Queenie takes Maude over and says, Maude, do you see a lovely and clever child here? and Maude goes up to that little one and rests her nose on his knee. It makes the boy smile and everything is fine and we can go on.

Queenie moves back to the centre and keeps announcing.

We have tumbling and juggling, also highwire. We have an eight-foot pedestal act and a comedy boxing act too. Here's Maude, our small horse, see how she tries to please! The clowns will make you laugh, she says, and then after all of that has left you breathless, it's our Grand Finale. The High Dive, performed by Miss Winnstay Gold. She will astound you with her courage, that's for sure.

Queenie doesn't much like overtalk, she says puffing is old-fashioned, that she's a plain-speaking woman with no need for those irritating frills. I see that about her and I get it but sometimes I think a person might like some frills, that there's nothing wrong with that.

—

Right before the clown act, Valentina will grab a handful of flour and tell Girl to shut her eyes and she'll throw it in her face and hair, and then I help her put her clown clothes on. Now do your clown laugh, Valentina says and Girl does and it comes out like a machine gun, just the way we taught her.

—

It's ninety minutes of non-stop action and we have to change costumes along the way. It might be Girl clowning solo while Valentina and I change into leotards for low-wire, or the engineer and Girl tumbling while I change for clowning. Us clowns, we can get our faces on in thirty seconds and off in almost the same time. The truck is fitted out with everything we need, and the wardrobe and other equipment are in baskets lined up in order. We pull out and dump in and move along until we're finished and it's the end of the show.

We rotate through the players and there are nine acts, ten if you count Maude. Sometimes she just wanders but there's one bit which is Girl hanging on to Maude's strap as she walks in big circles then Girl tries to get on but ends up the wrong way which means she's facing backwards and you might think it's too simple but it makes the audience happy.

Queenie does the talking in between. Sometimes she tries to tell a joke but it comes out a bit sad and people smile politely. I've seen it often, she can't manage to get them under her spell even though she does her best, we all do.

Then it's Valentina's skits, the playlets, the social commentaries she calls them. Compressed melodramas is how Queenie describes them. The bits about the small person fighting the regime and about landowners and merchants. We cover parenting, cheap imports, fast fashion, fast food. Homelessness and the tent cities and outbreaks of disease. The death of national manufacturing and excessive drinking and other social menaces. You might think these themes aren't fit for children but we camouflage them so all of it is hidden inside of the act. On the surface, the audience thinks we're being funny and simple and while we are that, what we also do is give them a message.

Valentina works in silence but Girl and I have easy lines and inside of those words are the hidden meanings. Valentina says there's power and meaning in silence but also in speech. Speaking and not speaking, both can be dangerous. We're clowns, she says, because what else can one be in a world such as this? That's what she says, that's what she thinks. The other thing she says is that a clown can get away with anything so we have to try.

—

We don't do violence against women. We don't ever do that, not even as a joke, not even as a tap on the bottom that makes a girl clown fall over. It's the small things that can build and they build over time, it's the small things you have to look out for.

—

Girl and I step to the edge of the ring and stand with our backs to the audience and we watch Valentina perform her solo and it's like ballet, she is that graceful. Her body tells stories and because it's mime, somehow it makes everything clear so that you can see what you're doing in your own life and what's good or bad about it. People afterwards, they stand at their cars too long and look at the sky. Or they're staring at the ground as they hold on to what it is that has made them feel so much in those moments during the show. And while they might think it's the rope act or the rings, or the sight of sweet Maude going in circles, or even the high dive that has touched them, I know it's Valentina. She reaches out and puts a hand on each person's shoulder and with that somehow she's gone inside them, she's made them feel something they didn't arrive with. I don't know how she does it, it's a kind of magic. What's the point of making people laugh if all you're doing is sending them back to their lives the same as before? she says. They need to be changed.

—

We do the fire bit, we worked it out the other day. We run around with our shoes that are too big, carrying buckets of water which is blue paper, and there are fake flames and a too-small hose and Girl bumps into me. She's carrying the bells, she's ringing them loud, and I fall and can't get up, my arms have no bones in them and my legs have no bones too and it's Valentina's job to help me. We both end up on the ground and Girl is standing over us, hands on hips with her laugh that she practised, it's high-pitched, it's a shriek, it's an alarm. A warning flare shot high into the sky from here to another place. It says, Look at us. See how we go on.

—

The boy who's a guy has a forehead that's wide, it makes him very manly that's all I can say. During interval, he comes to stand nearby as I do the lolly bags. He says he wants to buy one and says thanks when I pass it to him. He asks me how much and I point to the sign.

One dollar? he asks and I say, Yep.

He gives me the coin. Is that one okay?

I turn it over. Nope, I say, and pass it back.

He's smiling now as he gets another from his pocket and hands it across. I look at it closely. This one is fine, I say and put it in the tin. He's still looking at me but I don't smile. Even though I think I was trying to be funny and I think I want him to notice me, I'm not sure. I don't know what I'm doing and I don't know how I feel. It's possible I want to kiss him but it's also possible that I want him to go away.

—

Later, when it's right at the end of the show and I'm up the ladder, one spot is on me and the other on the tank, and the in-between is a dark stretch of space where anything could happen. That's when I look down on the audience and find where he's sitting. I let myself imagine he's worried about me, maybe even liking me. He thinks I'll fall off the back of the ladder and break my neck, my back, my head. Or that I'll slip and hit a rung on the way down. Or spin away from the pool and hit the ground dead.

He expects me to be scared and I do hesitate, I wait a long time before I go down. I step forward and back more than once, it's a good trick like Girl says. Inside, I'm strong and even though I think it's best that I am, sometimes I wish I could be that way about other things too, like about boys who are guys. Being on the ladder up in the night sky with a breeze on my face and my fingers itching, it's a moment when I come into my body as if for the first time.

The naphtha flares surge and the breeze, it's increasing, it's stronger now. I've decided, but the only thing I can think about is I have to dive before the wind builds much more, so I take a breath and go down fast into the night.

—

It's after the show and I hear Queenie. Her voice carries across the way.

Where's Win?

I don't know, Girl says. Her voice is loud as well.

I have to go, I say, and I come out of the darkness, walking fast.

Where were you? Girl asks.

I don't say anything. I push past her and go back into the light.

—

That night, I'm outside under the sky, under my heavy covers. It's cold, I can't sleep and I hear the others where they're sitting at the fire. I can't sleep, I can't even close my eyes, so I search the night for shapes to find, anything I can but there's nothing, only blackness. I touch my lips with my fingers. It feels like something has happened to me.

THE WOMAN

ANOTHER CAMP, A yellow neon sign out front: JESUS SAVES. We're in the eating tent, it's early evening and there's been an intake of sundowners, their bedrolls line the interior walls. Around us I hear mention of Paterson's Way and Wintermoon. Of how one man has been lately out on the Dumaresq River, and here we sit within a circular tide of people as they line for food and find a seat. For me, it's the stir of air that disturbs as others pass me by and the sensation is unpleasant. I wish we were on our own, out at the river. Those are the times I like best.

People help with the meal and all is as usual except for myself, because now there's a throb inside, like one of arousal but it's not that. It's not that. I will keep my stillness and tomorrow we will move on. We've covered a thousand people in the area and south is next, he's looking forward to the mushrooms. I'll be able to forage for some, he likes a mushroom cooked fresh over a fire. I'm pleased when I can make him pleased, it renders things easier.

One of the organisers comes and stands in front of us.

What is it you want? I ask.

There's a man here. Name of Willison. Wants to talk to the Reverend.

Let's talk to him, the Reverend says. We'll eat after.

We go out into the open where the man is standing by a car. As we draw near, with me walking in front, this Willison holds out his hand to me. I ignore it and he shakes the Reverend's hand. He's nervous.

On his part, there's no preamble, no circling of the matter.

Sorry to take you from your meal, he says.

It's no trouble.

Well, it's this. My sister recently found herself in a fix and she wanted to resume menses. He looks at his boots as he says these words and I look down too. The sharp-toed dress boots of the working rich.

She went out in the day, she lied to my brother-in-law. Said she was going to get her hair done.

He holds out a piece of paper, it looks like a pamphlet.

The Reverend puts his hand out for it. What's your name again?

It's Willison. Magnus.

Listen Magnus. What you let them get away with is what they continue with. Your brother-in-law has to show control in this instance. He should leave her, it will teach her a lesson. He could bring her to church, he could find another wife. Why is it you here and not the husband?

He's gone.

Well, if that's the case there's nothing I can do, if you understand me. Do you understand me, Mr Willison?

He says he does but there's other men. That there've been two others to vanish between here and the top river.

Disappeared?

That's right.

The Reverend spits sideways to the dirt. Men disappear, he says. They run off with other women, that's what the wives say. They're usually happy they've gone. It's the—how will I put it?—it's the problematic ones, is what I've heard.

Willison says, Of course, but this seems different. You haven't heard anything about men disappearing?

Well, let me think. There was one went for work in Dominance down south. He's the only one I know. Took his family with. But I'll ask around.

Sure, Willison nods.

They speak a while about the shuttle and what might be happening up there now, and then they talk about work. Willison is a butcher and they share a moment of connection. They talk of knives and where the best beef is farmed. How rare it is in these times to taste red flesh. The Reverend tells Willison that he's given up farmed meat, that nowadays he only consumes what is hunted or caught in the field. Willison says that even though there isn't much pastured meat, there is always call for a man who knows his knives. That the money is good.

It's a fine day when there is something fresh to cut, is it not? the Reverend says and Willison agrees.

I've a mind to share a story, he goes on and Willison waits.

There was a man who wrote an essay about eating infants. It was a long time ago.

Willison laughs. He thinks it's a joke and I find myself wanting to laugh too. I can't help myself and it pops as a small explosion out of my mouth. I dip my head to hide it but I know he's heard.

I haven't heard of such a thing, Willison says. Babies as food? It sounds strange, can't be true.

The man looks at me now. He senses what is in front of him, that there's something about the Reverend and it's true. While others might think his to be a smile that isn't heartfelt, I can say that he is entirely cold at the core. There's something stuck there from his early days, perhaps from boyhood. He told me his mother dressed him as a girl when he was little, that she beat him upon occasion. She was a dancer in the Hootchie Kootchie and it was a strong act, Pauline was her name. He found out about it later from a man who recognised him in the street and told him with a smirk what Pauline was. He called her hot stuff. A small boy, hanging around, playing marbles with other children, their fathers inside the tent. Children are meant to soften a person but she'd been hard so he'd struck out, once he was old enough. Struck out and trucked out, as they say. Left home to go on the road, away from all of that and it had saved him, is what he believes. But even so, all these years later, his mother is still with him and always has been, and in a way she will never leave. I heard this as I was lying on the ground with his boot in my stomach. He was crying as he told me.

As a satire, the Reverend is saying. He wrote other things, he was an Anglican cleric too. Imagine! A man of God writing such a thing. Anyone writing such a thing.

Willison agrees. Strange, he says.

They say their goodbyes and the man leaves.

Did you hear that? he says to me. Interesting, but let's eat, I'm hungry. I follow him back to the tent.

—

I'm sitting with a plate in front of me, it's a meagre serving of tinned three beans and mayonnaise potatoes when suddenly he is there. He's finished and he gestures for me to follow him outside. He takes me from the back flap of the tent and I notice a small part of the sky, how beautiful it is, with the rare blue of an Araucana egg. I'm holding my plate, he wants to be gentle but he can't manage it. Someone has said something to him, or maybe it was the laugh he heard at the same time as Willison's.

However it's come to be, instantly it's upon him, it's in him. He slaps my plate to the ground. He grabs my neck and squeezes for a time before he lets go. We're leaving in an hour, he says. Get the car ready.

—

As I wash my hands down by the river I think I hear a bird singing. It's a strange sound, out of time. It reminds me of girlhood and my brother's collection of nests. How patient he had to be until he knew the bird had gone. Only then would he climb up to claim it and sometimes I'd help him, sometimes I'd go up to get a nest too. He taught me the names of birds and about their eggs. Whenever we found one broken on the ground, we stopped and said a prayer. My brother was gentle, he was a good person.

I go to the car, to wait. He arrives.

Get in, he says. Why am I always waiting for you?

We leave and there is silence for hours after that.

WIN

IT'S ME AND the clown up front with Queenie and Girl in the back and the engineer is driving the Merc. We're on the way to Riverside and in the back of the truck Queenie sits in her wraps, even though it isn't very cold. I look around to check and see her eyes are open, her face flat, not so tough now. Her back has been a trouble to her since she fell from a horse. It was a long time ago, when they made the ring from sandbags and had proper sawdust but even so the horse slipped. We make a ring, Valentina calls it the circle. These days we mark it out with a rope, we dig it out a bit, it helps Maude go better. We don't want her to be on grass, it gets greasy and that's when she might slide. We have to take care of Maude, she's the last horse left.

Queenie's back is so bad some mornings she can barely move. I feel like a sitting duck is what she said the other day.

No one's trying to shoot you, I said.

She pointed to a silo out the window. Look at that, Win, thousands of tonnes of grain. By the time your body was found you'd be dried out completely unless the mice got to you first. Queenie knows about silos. She's out of the flour mills down south.

—

She's had lots of jobs on the show. Tickets and the books, and she did routes and food, she did all of that as well as perform. She had an emerald belt and drove an eight-horse hitch all stallions. It broke her when they had to butcher them, it happened one by one to help feed the lions, but then the law changed and they had to shoot the cats as well, they put them in a pit out back at Arcadia. They shot them then burned them and the elephants too. They're in the same ground, their bones all mixed together and like I said, we only have Maude and Pet now, they're the last ones.

Queenie did reclamations all the way through from before she joined the show but she tells me it's different now, that women are more desperate. Even though she was tough in the ring, she was the soft one who'd sit with the women, not Pearl. The ones who needed a bit longer, a few minutes before they could leave the van and go back to their lives.

—

We stop for lunch. It must be near the middle of the day and we're having puftaloons, which makes Girl happy. I tell her we might be able to find black plums and that makes her happy as well. We get out and the engineer goes to the front of the truck, she's doing something with the left headlight, a stone must have hit it she thinks. She says if we have to travel at night, we can't do it with one light when it's dark and not only because of kangaroos. I get what she means. She has a gun it's a long one, a rifle. I know where she keeps the bullets. I know how to use the smaller one too because she showed me. You probably can't imagine a girl my age with a gun but I'm not a bad shot.

Enough of that, we have daytime eating to do. I can smell the fire and today it's rabbit, my favourite even with all the bones.

—

The road we're on follows a line of trees but soon we're out the other side and from then it's open pasture, and after that there are more rounded hills and a small mountain as well. The landscape is folded with fossil dunes curved over and rocks split by frost, they're not as strong or permanent as you might think. A large cut-out section looms ahead, it's a mine, Valentina says. A new one. They've got thermal and semi-soft coking coal, she adds, and I don't know what you think of that but all of us, we hate it. It's that sort of thing that has killed the world.

—

It's an hour later when our tyre goes. Queenie is agitated, she thinks we won't have enough time for set-up. We're stopped again by the road and I'm bored as anything when the men come, they appear too quickly for us to get inside. They park and walk to us and stand with their arms crossed. There's three of them, two are big, they're brothers they say, and I think it's strange they tell us that because why would we care? The other is a boy, he's hunched over with pocks in his skin and I'm wondering to myself if I would kiss him. They ask if we have any water we can spare and the engineer goes to fill their bottle. One of the brothers starts telling a story about where they're going. He speaks of a man, he says he destroyed his life, that he'd never done anything wrong until he did do one small wrong which led to a bigger one. The man's voice starts to go funny, it trembles and that's when I know he's been drinking and Queenie must have known it too because she puts her hand up and says, Girls come inside and help me and we go into the truck and shut the door. Queenie motions with a finger to her lip for me to slide the bolt so I do.

We're in the truck and I'm annoyed, it means I can't see if the boy will notice me but Queenie is boss and I imagine her voice if she knew what I was thinking. Oh, Win, she'd say. Don't be ridiculous. I can hear the man through the window and Queenie is telling Girl to get a book to read to her, she's been teaching her letters but I stay near the door.

The man is saying that he hadn't seen it for himself, how could he? It started when he was a child and it was gradual. He had a sister, she was younger and he couldn't see her as a person of equal value to him. And with time it became about the boy and his behaviour. I press my face at the window and I can see the other two looking away. They don't like the man telling the story but he doesn't notice or he doesn't care, he keeps talking. He'd go out to drink, he goes on, and would come back and he still didn't realise this sister was a whole other person. These feelings, he didn't know where they came from, they were not of him, not there to begin with, he was sure of that. It wasn't his fault but the thing was the girl, and her importance, and this was what he'd come to see too late. She'd become forgotten by everyone.

So you see, he says, no one thought about her. It had taken him all this time to know that it was her at the centre all along but at the same time it was she who was forgotten, who didn't count. She stayed that way until recently, when she left that invisible centre, he says. She up and took herself off and they were on their way to her funeral now.

After they left, Valentina says, What was that about? Clear as mud. And she laughs, but Queenie says, He was the bad man. He was talking about himself. It was about him and his sister.

How'd you get that from his little speech?

It was in his eyes. He's angry not guilty and he blames her. I should have offered him a free shave.

We pass the cemetery down the road. They're gathered and I see the men, they're standing. I think about that sister and the man and what it was that he was telling us. He'd been drunk and his words unclear but that man, all he cared about was his own pain. How what had happened made him feel bad and that meant he wasn't able to think of himself as a good person. You could tell he wanted to have that. It's something people need, even the worst ones. They need to believe they're good even when they know they're not.

—

Queenie says she needs to go to town and that I'll have to take her.

I don't want to, I say I'm busy, I'm sewing my swimming cap. She wants me to come with, she doesn't like being alone. She says we have to and so I say, Alright. What do you need? Meaning which shop are we going to because now I'm thinking I'd like to look at some tops. I don't have many clothes and my tops are too loose, I'd like something fitted, something maybe that goes down a bit more in front.

We need flour and salt, she says. Let's go.

I get behind the wheel of the Merc and wait for Queenie.

I'm thinking it might be almost my time to stop, she says, as soon as she has her seatbelt on. I look out at the road, it's a good one, it's sealed.

I say I'll think about it but she says, What's there to think? It is what it is. I'm coming to the end and you need to take over.

—

It's only when we're driving back with the flour and salt that I realise I didn't see any tops. We've passed the aerodrome and the aquaculture when she brings up the next thing. She wants me to do a new tank act called Obelia which will be me eating and smoking under the water. That'll be the effect, she says. We'll need the engineer to figure out how to build a tank with clear sides but before I can ask how do I smoke a cigarette under water we're almost at the bridge and she makes a noise.

Oh, she says.

I see what she's talking about. It's a group of cars down by the river and people are putting up a tent and others are organising stoves and tables and chairs.

Looks like a meeting. They're going to run a service, Queenie says.

We drive on and neither of us speak for a bit and then she says, It's religion. Best to steer well clear of anyone like that.

THESE ARE OUR days, they go past all the same. We sew and drive and perform and reclaim. We read the signs and talk about how to be better clowns. If we have a show and there are lollies to sell, I take the coins and hand over the bags, and if I'm on tickets it's the same. We travel all the roads and the billboards tell us something of the world beyond. ELECTIONS—SHOPPING CENTRES—HEALTH CARE—THE SHUTTLE PROGRAM—NEW TV SERIES—$400 EXORCISMS—RELIGION—TAROT—PALM-READING—POLITICIANS—THE ALLIANCE—SPORT and now the new ones saying PRAY FOR THE ASTRONAUTS. None of it seems real, it's very far from our lives. I find I'm not caring about acts or reclamations. I don't care about the astronauts dying up there, not even the dog. I don't care about sewing a new swim cap or the high dive or elephants or pineapples either. Queenie has told me she wants to stop and that means it's going to be me.

—

It's after tea and proper dark and Girl asks the clown if she's married. She asks the engineer too and they look at each other and the clown says, Well not to each other and the engineer laughs and then Valentina gets up and does a dance and sings, 'Here Comes the Bride'.

Then Girl says to Queenie, What about you? Where's your husband? Did you love him a lot?

He was alright, he was fine, Queenie says. Frank Gold was a good person and I knew it as soon as I laid eyes on him. He was one of the sons of Mr Gold, who was the boss. Frank used to say a third husband didn't need to hear about the other two that came before and I always thought, Well, that's fine, but I'll tell you. Number one, you don't want to know. Number two, he was in pubs. Then the next thing, two dies and three walks into the bar. Mr Frank Gold he calls hisself, and I give him a beer and he gets a bit sozzled. On the one! Never was much of a drinker and that's what sold me. A man that doesn't drink? Where do I sign up?

Everyone jokes about running away with the circus but I can't understand anyone not wanting to be with the show. He was romantic but shy, you know the type. I'd look at those eyes and wonder he wasn't one of them hypnotisers, they put you in a trance and get control of your mind and tell you to take off your knickers, excuse my.

Yuck, says Girl.

But I was newly widowed—twelve months—and keeping to m'self as you should under those circumstances, so I didn't even look this duffer full in the face until he asked me to the river. I had my back turned and overheard him tell another bloke he was going to marry me. Standing at the bar he was so darned straight and wide in his shirt, with a little curl of hair above the top button where his throat dipped, I remember that. I had my conditions which I laid out for him. I had them writ down and I read from the list, it was a short list mind you. I don't remember now what it was, probably about beatings and that. We went to the river, he was leaving and I wouldn't see him for another year and I didn't know how I felt about that, I wasn't happy I can tell you that much. We went for a picnic and Frank'd brought a blanket and sandwiches, and he's put the rug down and I sit and he sits and we eat. He doesn't talk very much but then neither do I. We're right on the bend of the Ovens, by a broken gum tree. We had our picnic when blow me down the small conversation we'd been struggling to have dries up. He'd been talking about permits and I'd been saying, Mmm, interesting, even though it weren't very and then he stops talking, he flat-out stops, and I think to myself, Oh, here we go. So I swallow what I was going to say. I'd been casting about, trying to think of something to get us going again and I was probably going to talk about the weather, how dry it had been all year, and I'm going to ask him whether he had a preferred season, when all of a sudden he opens his mouth and says, One hundred and fifty licences, that's what you need now. Each licence has its own particulars and costs associated, makes it nigh impossible, and I'm about to say, What are you going on about? when he asks me to marry him. I say, Hang on a minute. Let a girl catch her breath. He takes my hand and he goes, We don't have much time, we're moving on, and I'm thinking, Good lord, when just then, down the river, comes a sight the likes I'd never had and I've been to the Moomba parade and everything. Like a barge it was, a sort of dray I suppose you'd call it but not with wheels. It was made of wood and floating down the river and on top of it were two dogs and a pony. Turned out that pony was Toby. Smallest horse in the country, smaller than Maude even. He could count up to twenty-five and do simple sums. The dogs were both terriers, they belonged to Miss Mimi who I was going to meet in thirty minutes. But all of that was simply the beginning of it, and if you thought a pony floating down a river on planks of wood tied together was strange enough then you've got another think coming.

Next it was Cleopatra. Now that was the sight. Her colour as she came nearer shifted with the light of the sun through the trees, and I can tell you I've never seen anything as beautiful as it in all my days. People think elephants are grey but they're not. Their skin changes and her colour at that moment was purple. She moved down the river, following the others, water to her shoulders. Frank whistles to her, he calls out and she pushes the raft with the dogs and the pony to the bank and they get off and then Cleo starts to climb out of the water. Well, I can tell you I was equal parts exhilarated and terrified and nothing much shakes this old bird.

Do you like animals? Frank asks me then.

And she steps right out, the elephant does. She gets up onto the bank and her legs are that big. She comes over to us, she gets so close I can see how long her eyelashes are—like *this*—and Frank gives her a sandwich.

I do like animals, I say, hoping to get him back to the thing that was on his mind, which was a proposal.

He smiles. Alright then, he says. Good. And he offers me another sandwich.

Just then, Cleo puts the end of her trunk on top of my head and other girls might've been upset, with their hair getting mussed, but I wasn't, I was never like that. The weight of it resting there was very reassuring which you'll probably think a lot of tripe. And we sit there with the dogs at our feet, they're sleeping on their sides, dear little pets, panting a bit with the heat. The pony is standing over near a tree.

Then Frank asks me again and I say yes. I say yes, I will go with him the day after and yes I will marry him. I said I had two conditions, I remember them now. One was that he was never to lay a hand on me, that if he did he wouldn't get a second chance, I'd be gone. He agrees to that.

And the second was that when I sold the hotel, I wouldn't give him any of the money and he says that was acceptable.

Then he has a question for me and it was the one I'd been dreading, about children. He tells me his grandmother produced a baby every second year, which was fifteen though not all survived, of course, there was the war on and that. But big families are good for the show, he says. The trifecta, if you like, is a woman who can perform, manage and bear children. I say that I'm already on the old side. I'm thirty-five, I tell him, thinking this will do it, this will break it and he'll say goodbye.

She looks at me. Girl's asleep, I say, and Queenie goes on.

Never mind that, Frank tells me. He'd be happy with whatever I was able to bring forth from my fundamental reproductive area—that's how he put it—and while I thought that was a bit risqué and not at all romantic, I let it pass. I held on to his hand, I gripped him hard because now I was realising how much I did want to go on the road with his company, with the elephants, but I had to tell him, I couldn't not, so I said it.

I can't have children, I say. Just like that. Infection, I say.

But I didn't have to worry. He squeezes my hand and says it's fine. He tells me he had the mumps and his brother did too, that we might well be the last generation of Golds but what can you do?

I asked him later how long he'd planned all of that but he wouldn't say. The man was quiet in regular life. He'd sit there like nobody's and keep it shut, but once he was in the ring he could talk the leg off a chair.

I joined the show. I cooked for them all, sewed and mended and taught the younger ones some sums. I helped feed the animals, I rode Cleo, I did the takings, handled the money and checked the weather forecasts. I kept the rogues in hand. But when I went to my caravan of a night, all I wanted was a quiet cup of tea, perhaps a nice biscuit or two, and then sleep. We all got on, show people need to stick together. There's families upon families and that's not only in the aerial stacks. Even if the blood running through me is different to the blood running through the animal trainer or the unicyclist or juggler it doesn't matter. We all needed each other and that hasn't changed any I don't think. The young ones grew up and a lot of them left but we stayed on, we kept it going.

I do miss my Frank. He made me laugh. The way he'd talk about tea: *Endows a man with fortitude, aptitude and staves off decrepitude. Increases likeability, credibility and agility. Plausibility. It would not be an understatement of factual veracity to affirm that this tea here might serve to extend the quality of vivacious existence. And do you take juice of the bovine variety? Granules of the sweet green fields of upright woody growth material oft used in furniture making and of the gardenous nature?* What a ringmaster he was, with that talk he was marvellous, the best puffer I ever heard, and he was the only one who ever made me laugh.

Queenie gets up slowly. But those days are over, she says. Time for bed.

—

Valentina had a bad husband that's why she's with us. One day he took Valentina and threw her out of the house, he locked the door against her and wouldn't open it. He left her standing outside and she had no clothes on, she was naked. She had to beg at the window, beg for him to let her back in to get clothes but he wouldn't. A neighbour came and gave her a blanket.

When Valentina told me this story she said he had laughed at her when he finally let her back in the house. He called her ugly and said that he didn't love her anymore. I couldn't believe it because Valentina is beautiful. When she dances in the show she wears a leotard and tights and rubs glitter on her face. When the light catches her hair and her lips all of it is dark and magic. She twists and bends through space and in that moment I want to be her. I want to have that hair and that face. After Valentina dances, when I come to do my high dive it feels different, it feels as if my energy is less because Valentina is a person who has had men love her but she's a woman who has left them behind.

I wonder what it's like to say no to love, to leave it all behind.

IT'S NOT A heartbeat is what I understand and the people who say it is are making a mistake because what they're talking about as a beat is just electrics. It's a stub where the heart will grow but they want to say 'heart' instead of 'electrical impulses' and they want to say 'feelings' instead of 'inability to experience pain' and they always say 'baby' instead of 'foetus' because the truth isn't as useful to them as being able to persuade people. A foetus is alive at six weeks, twelve weeks, eighteen weeks of course it is but it won't live outside the womb so how can they give it rights? People don't want to admit that there's no ability to survive, well the woman can but not what's growing inside. And that's the other bit. They only say 'mother' rarely 'woman' and never ever 'person with a uterus'.

—

Once I asked Queenie if she was frightened of angry husbands.

I'm not scared of them, she said. Angry husbands are my speciality. Why should a man decide whether his wife can go to the doctor or not? Whether she can visit her family? If she can wear trousers? If she can use contraception? How to vote? No, you can bring me all of those angry husbands and I'll show them what it feels like to be at the mercy of someone stronger and smarter. I'll show them how it feels to be unsafe, if only for the second that it takes them to realise what's happening as their blood begins to run free. They'll be sorry then, they'll be sorry but it will be too late.

—

When the women come to us, sometimes they cry while they wait. I take them in and sit them down and we try to make them feel better. Queenie explained to me how to do it.

Don't pat them for too long like they're dogs but do put your hands on them. It helps them feel less alone.

She sits them down and says, A fresh look will make all the difference.

I don't want to pretend that all of them are upset because that would be a lie. Some of them arrive calm with their faces straight. Some are cold about it while others feel bad afterwards, but if they don't feel bad they feel relieved. Some of them do want it, the pregnancy that is, but they can't have it, they can't have the baby. Queenie tells them that a person can feel lots of things at the same time and that's okay. That's the word she uses. It's okay, she says over and over. She knows that emotions can clash and layer across the top of other feelings. That sometimes you're numb for a while and then it comes later, the reaction that is, it can be a long while later, even years. It might be grief, it might be sadness but all of it is okay, she says. However you feel. But in the moment, this moment, you need it done and we're here to help. That's what she says as well.

The world is filled with different types, she said to me. There's more than three. Forget about what Valentina says, forget about clowns. Something like this goes beyond right and wrong, it's beyond good and evil, and that's when I said, But you told me there's no right or wrong about it, and she says, Well there is, pet, there is a right and there is a wrong but with this you have to go past it. You'll see one day, you'll understand that really, in the end, this is beyond all of that.

But the problem is I'm not sure I will understand, that I will ever understand it myself.

—

She's been running the service for a long time. She did reclamations when she was young. After her experience, she learned how to do them for others and how to do them better. Safer. It's been around forever because as long as men have been impregnating women there have been unwanted babies. Half the pregnancies in the world aren't planned. She told me that when I was starting and I found it hard to believe.

Think about that is what she said. And I did.

IT'S LATE AFTERNOON. We've left Girl and Valentina at a BP, it has a restaurant and Girl has colouring pencils and a book. We don't want to stop long we still have a way to go, and I carry some chairs and set them up under a tree. Queenie and I, we wait there while the engineer boils the kettle then we have tea and bread with jam.

I expect this one might cause us trouble, Queenie says. Her face is serious. It's him I'm worried about, she goes on.

She's talking about the father, she's talking about Mr Bode. I look at the engineer and she looks at me and we're both thinking the same thing, which is that Queenie is always right. She predicted the big tent blow-down in '96 and the next one that happened in '15. She's been right about all those times and other things too. When Queenie says she has a feeling, everybody listens.

—

Back in the truck on our way again and we're almost asleep, that's us two, me and Queenie. The engineer is awake, she never gets in a trance on the road. A billboard flashes by, it's a photo of a man, he has a beard and angry eyebrows and a leather strap tied around his head. NEED A BOUNTY HUNTER? CALL MAX and then the number. The engineer makes a noise. It's from a film, she says. An old film.

A bit later and we see up the road a new camp of Saviours. They're all white, their clothes and skin and tents and vans, everything is white.

Queenie doesn't want us to ever speak with these people. She said if I come across them to leave it to her. And if I'm not with you, she says, walk away. This settlement we're passing now is a big one, it stretches the length of half a kilometre or more so we have to slow right down. There are tents near the road and wooden shacks with painted walls, the words of people hard done by. I read their rants about God and their statements of history and claim and explanation: IF I AM WRONG YOU CAN ARREST ME I AM READY FOR THAT.

There are a lot of people living there and children come out to run beside the truck.

Queenie calls me to come in back, she's awake now.

More and more children run out to follow us and then there's a loudspeaker on the road behind, it's a man and we hear his voice.

Hail, fellow Australians, why not join us for a prayer!

Queenie calls to the engineer. Don't you stop, keep going, and the engineer says, Of course, and we drive slowly past the waving children.

I look through the rear window.

What is it? Queenie asks.

It's that man, the one who came. He's on the road.

The one with the hat?

Yes, the one who came to camp.

Keep back, she says. Hopefully he doesn't recognise the truck. But I know he will. I remember his eyes, looking around our lot.

As we pass on down the road, the man behind us puts the bullhorn to the side of his leg and watches us. I see the woman with her white headdress, she's holding her tambourine its pale blue ribbons floating in the breeze. The children stop running. They gather around the man and he holds his arms wide as they stomp and spin in their white clothes. He's facing our way, he doesn't move and neither do I until I can't see him in the road anymore.

—

Mr Bode, well Queenie can't stand him. She's sorry for his wife, who's a mother of five not counting bits and pieces. We're sorry for his daughters too. I've seen him a few times and it was his eyes I didn't like and the way that if you talk to his daughters he comes and stands too close, it makes you feel strange. Why does he care what girls talk about?

I like the sisters, all five of them. There's Derla, Alda and Roslin, they're my age and a bit younger, and then there's Twinnie and Bip who are the younger ones. They've been to our shows but not lately.

—

The engineer pulls into a clearing ten kilometres this side of the town sign. She opens the annexe, sets up the salon for the haircuts with two chairs and a mirror. She does that first then gets the other equipment out of the truck. I put the sign out but away from the road, we don't want random people stopping. HAIRCUTS & STYLES it says: $15 and PENSIONERS FREE and then I sit and wait. Queenie is still in the back, I can hear her moving about getting things ready. The bed is there and the desk lamp and the kettle. The masks and aprons and green rubber sheeting. The towels and the dilators and scrapers. She uses a single-blade speculum, it looks like a hair-curling wand. When I pointed that out to her she said, Of course, Win. That's why I use it. A double-blade, its function is clear but not this one. This one we can say it's for hair.

The engineer starts a fire on the other side, away from the truck, it's a small one but we can boil the billies a few times over and with flame enough to get rid of the beginnings. Queenie used to keep the scraps, she kept them in the freezer chest and would take them back to Arcadia to bury them, she thought it was safer. But she got worried about wild dogs digging, we have more of those now. She told me if I ever need to bury anything to make sure I put a big stone on top, something heavy to stop the animals getting at it. Be sure to dig it deep, she said.

She told me when she goes herself she hopes to be able to think of nice things in the moment: her grandmother's steak-and-kidney pie, a lamb being born, pressing flowers between thick pieces of paper. But let's not talk about these things now, she said. They're for later. Let's not think about that now.

—

We're on the dark side of the road, in a clearing with heavy trees all round. The engineer doesn't say anything but she's always checking, always listening, and I'd guess she's imagining the father. How he'd crash through the bush, maybe with a gun. The engineer's strong and has a thick neck. Like I said, she used to be the lion person, I think that's why her eyes are everywhere at once. She still has the cage and whips and her waistcoat with the gems sewn on, they're all in storage now.

Soon there's the sound of a car in the distance so we go inside and the engineer waits out front. Down the road comes a long brown car. Someone wearing white gloves is holding the wheel which makes me think it's the mother and it is. It's

Mrs Bode. She's getting out of the car, she's going around to the back door. She opens it and then I see one of her girls. Queenie is walking to the car fast and she's calling to me so I follow.

Help her, Win. Come on. She puts her hands on the girl. Too hot, she says. The girl is making noises. It's Bip.

It's alright, let's just have a look at you. Bring her inside, Queenie says, and the engineer picks Bip up. I get the blanket and Queenie tells me to put it over her, so I do that. I put it over Bip.

Mrs Bode and I follow.

Bip's the second-last, she's thirteen now I think. Her face is shiny and white and her mouth is open and she could be singing but no sound comes out, no sound at all. The engineer takes her inside and puts her on the bed and then Queenie is there with her hand on Bip's forehead.

I can tell this isn't good.

Have her sit down there, Queenie says over her shoulder, down in the salon, so I take Mrs Bode's arm and I show her the cutting chair and when she sits she says, Thank you.

Our person will bring you a cup of tea, I say.

Mrs Bode says alright. Her head is covered in tightly wound curls, I bet she does them with rags at night.

I listen to the sound of Queenie's voice murmuring inside and I hear her saying, I need to check you love, and Bip is saying, No, I don't want you to.

Did she do something to herself? Queenie is at the doorway and she's talking to Mrs Bode who looks up and says, I think so, yes. I said we'd come to you. I told her to wait. But she was upset of course, she didn't want anybody to find out. Is she going to be alright?

Queenie says she doesn't think so. She says that we should all be worried and get ready for the worst. She said that last bit in a whisper not wanting Bip to hear. It's when they put things inside of themselves, Queenie says. Things that aren't clean or things that are too sharp, they can put a hole in there you know. It's delicate. When bacteria gets in or there's a perforation it can be serious and that's when I can't do anything.

A perforation?

It's a tear, a hole, Queenie says. It's that.

Come up now, Queenie says to me, and we begin. I'm at the lower end and Queenie up top. She's holding the girl's head, she's telling her to keep still. Let Win have a look, she needs to have a look. We might need to change positions, she says to me, but see how you go.

Bip is on the bed, her head moving side to side. Her stomach is flat but her skin, it's yellow from the waist down and there's a smell. When I look inside of her with the light I can see her cervix, I can see there's a broken needle half out of it, grey and flat. It's for crochet, one with a hook, it's one of those.

Is it worth dilating? Queenie asks, and I shake my head.

Oh, she says. Is it the puerperal?

I nod. It's because of the smell. There's nothing we can do, what she needs is to go to a hospital but they won't do that and we know it. We can give her something for the fever, maybe they'll be able to get antibiotics, or a serum even, it's expensive and old-fashioned but that's all they might be able to do.

I close Bip's legs and walk around to her head. Her eyes are closed and she's stiff with dots of sweat on her top lip. Soon she'll start shaking and go into shock, I'm surprised she hasn't already.

I'll talk to her mother, Queenie says. You have a word to Bip.

I put my finger on Bip's crucifix where it rests at her throat. Did you tell your mum? I ask.

She rolls her head from side to side and says she would rather die.

That's probably going to happen anyhow, I say. You should tell her, you have to think of your sisters.

Leave me alone. I don't care and she doesn't do anything anyway.

He won't stop, I say. I don't know how I understand this but I do, I feel it in my body and I couldn't be more certain. She knows who I'm talking about.

I get her some water and we sit her in the chair, it's down the back near the window. I put a shawl around her and kneel down in front to massage her feet.

Why are you being kind to me? she asks as I take her shoes off.

Do you remember we played once? You were little, it was after the show and they let you and your sisters come and watch us tear down. You fell over and sat down in some of Maude's dung and cried. I picked you up and put you on my hip and carried you for a while. I pretended you were my baby. I was little myself maybe I was ten, it was a long time ago.

I mean why are you being kind to me now?

It's not your fault, I say. It's never the girl's fault. We want to help.

Help, she says. I suppose.

—

We put Bip back in the car and Mrs Bode says thank you. She gives Queenie money and they leave.

She won't make it, Queenie says. It will be terrible. We bow our heads, including the engineer.

Later we heard Bip died, it took two days. I remembered what Queenie had said. That it would take time and would be terrible. I knew it wasn't my fault, that there was nothing we could do but I felt awful for Bip all the same.

THE WOMAN

ANOTHER TENT, AND then another. We're ready to leave and get back on our way. We're sitting waiting for the man to come with the money. Eventually he arrives and he tells us there is someone to see the Reverend.

You can bring him, the Reverend says. These husbands, he turns to me. These men who cannot manage their families.

I hear the wind is still up, it's jangling at my nerves and maybe his too, because something makes him swear then and it's a word I've never heard him use.

Two people are brought to the chairs in front of us, a man and a girl. The little one wears a cotton dress and has skinny legs. She's about nine but maybe she's small for her age, who can tell these days. What's clear is the man is angry. It comes off him as heat and the girl is feeling it as well because she's holding on to his arm, she pulls it around her shoulder and clasps his hand as they sit across the way. The man is balding and clean-shaven though not very well. Hooded eyes and a mouth become wet with spittle. This is someone whose attention you do not want to draw so I hold myself as still as I can.

It takes a few minutes for him to calm enough to speak. He tries several times but his voice fails and he falls into a coughing fit. He accepts a drink of water and manages to say he's sorry. He's that upset, he says, and he probably shouldn't have come but was urged by his conscience and so came he did.

At the mention of conscience, the Reverend sits up.

You hear that, Sister? he says. Did I not mention conscience in my sermon just now? He decides to listen to this man. He likes the idea of signs.

Tell me your concern, he says. He shifts forward so he can touch the man if he needs. Sometimes it requires a hand to encourage a loosening. Lay a hand on them and they open, is what he told me.

It's one of my daughters, the man says. Another one. This is my youngest. This here is Twinnie.

And what is your name, sir? The Reverend puts his hand on the man's where it rests on his knee. It's a fleeting touch and I'm sure he doesn't feel the repulsion that I do, it's usually a matter of gender.

Ignatius Bode, Reverend. I have five daughters but I'm here about my Bip. She's left us, she's gone. Only thirteen. A good girl, very pretty and clean.

The Reverend sits back in his chair.

She died. I can't believe it. So beautiful, the most lovely skin of them all.

The Reverend makes a noise. He and I know what's going on here, the mention of skin quality, it's a tell as clear as in a game of poker.

Bode dips his head, his fury is clear to me and to the Reverend now I'm sure.

And your wife?

She's at home with the others.

Tell me what happened to your daughter.

She did something to herself. She couldn't have the child. Bode passes a hand over his face. His other arm is still across Twinnie's shoulders and the girl takes his wrist and slips his thumb into her mouth. Bode pulls his hand away but we see it.

She has sinned then, the Reverend says. She has paid for it.

Bode nods. She tried to do it by herself first, she put something inside of her, but she fell ill, a bad fever. That's when my wife took her to a woman. I heard about it after, it took a while to find out what had happened. So many lies.

A woman?

On the road. She travels, she does these operations.

Do you know where she is now?

I might, says Bode. They move around the place like I said but I know some of the spots.

What can you tell me about them?

She's old. They do performances, circus tricks. She's a hairdresser too. I thought that was all she did but she does the other as well.

The Reverend looks at me. He stands and it's swift so I do too.

I will find this woman, the Reverend tells Bode. But for you, all I will say is get your house in order.

He tells me to take them out. Come with me, I say. I don't want to be near the man and I'm trying not to look at the girl. This is the shame, this is what's at the centre of everything. We see, we understand, but we do nothing.

The girl is holding her father's hand again, they're walking to their car. I want to get them into it, I want to watch them leave. But first, I will do this. I want to make sure he hears me, so I speak clearly.

Hi there, I say. Where is your place in all of it?

Bode stops. Around us, the pallid light of the day and him dark as mud at the centre.

It's not me who's done wrong here.

What I mean is what is your part in this? With your daughters?

He casts about, he doesn't have any words. I think he is shocked that a woman is daring to speak to him in this way. The Bible says— he begins.

The Bible says all sorts of things that do not pass for right these days. 'None of you shall approach to any that is near of kin to him, to uncover their nakedness. I am the Lord.' Yes, it does not specify daughters, yes, Leviticus talks around it, but we know what it means. Everyone knows.

He won't look me in the eye.

You'd better go now, I say.

He gets into the car and it's how he puts his hand on his daughter's shoulder. There is something in the touch that rouses me.

Hi there, I say again. I rap the window and he puts it down.

I lean into the car, I put my face up close to his. I speak softly so the girl won't hear.

If you sleep with your daughters you will stop now.

He starts to speak.

You do sleep with your daughters?

He swallows and this is my answer.

His hand goes to the ignition.

You will join all of them in hell but it's you who will have put them there.

I straighten and watch as he drives away.

—

It's only once we are on the road that my breathing begins to regulate.

A hairdresser, he says. The show people, they tricked us. I will kill that fucking hag.

Lately I've wondered. I've thought he was almost at the end of it, that he was almost out of caring, but now I see there might be something left for an old woman, for an old show woman who has dared lie to his face.

WIN

IT'S OUR SECOND-LAST day and we're going down an old highway, it's narrow and runs along the river. Queenie's map calls it the eastern route, it's where the show used to go but back in those days they took the good roads while we stay on the bad ones. As I said before, we like how they're empty, how you can drive half a day and see no one. Queenie likes it and Girl likes it a lot, and even though the engineer says it's not good for the tyres Queenie says that's the way we go.

—

Six-thirty every morning, that's when Queenie appears from her sleeping compartment and pauses on the step. She sniffs the air and gives her proclamation: Rain/No rain. She can smell fire too, most of us can, of course we worry about that a lot and wind too after that, and even though rain isn't dangerous for the show it makes everything hard. You can't walk and you can't keep things clean. You can't lie on your back in a meadow to look at the sky and smell the grass. There are other things we can't do but that's because of superstition. We can't wear green or play the harmonica or set up tent on a Friday, don't ask me why because I'll say I don't know. Because Queenie says, that's why.

She said no rain today but she has a headache and it comes from the wind, she says it's the foehn. We're downside the Range now, it's the one place she hates to visit but we go every year because the earnings are better, not much but a bit. It's a place where psychosis comes close and people need distractions, she says, they need relief, and I didn't know what she meant until this year. Now is the first time I've felt something going on in my head too.

Queenie met a woman once. She reclaimed her, and as she sat with her cup of tea afterwards the customer said that none of us can ever know how close we are to madness, which means that any one of us can tip to the other side in a quick hot moment. Queenie said she didn't believe it and I said I didn't either.

But the devil-wind, she says, it gets inside you and changes your thinking. It makes you question everything. She said that, so maybe we do believe, we just don't want to admit it to ourselves.

—

There's a painting in three parts and the third panel has a hurdy-gurdy, the third panel is hell, it's filled with greys, reds and blacks. There's a pig in a nun's outfit, a hare, a dice, birds flying out of someone's backside near a bleached skull. A moth, a set of ears with a blade in the middle, a key, a lantern, a boat. Ladders that go nowhere, a hangman's scaffold, armies and flags. It's like one of Girl's dreams she tells us about, with monsters, half-human and half-animal. Girl talks about thick black stuff which covers everything in the world and makes the whole of it and us dark. All of it and all of us. I don't know the painting but Valentina does, she saw it in a book when she was young and she's never forgotten how it made her feel. She told us about it one night at dinner and Girl listened and then fell asleep and maybe that's where the monsters came from. You don't forget something like that, I mean the type of dream that wakes you up and makes you breathe hard.

—

It's dry for now but the sky has a quality as Queenie calls it. If it rains we have the tarps and sometimes I choose to sleep out beneath a piece of canvas, it's thick and good to be under especially when the wind is high and you can hear the dry trees falling in the distance. Those have been my best times.

I like to be outside on a blanket with another above and a section of tent right on top of all. With my eyes closed it's time to smell the old sawdust and horsehair and think of what it is that I want for myself.

When I'm out there I try to block the grown-ups' voices if they're nearby. They talk about when they were young, the Florida Apartments on the Gold Coast where they wintered each year, before they got the canning factory. They talk about how those were the best days, about the games of Mahjong and Miss Mimi and doing handstands in the hallways. Those are the things they talk about but I don't really listen, it's not interesting to me anymore. Girl likes to hear all of the stories, they're new for her, but I want to lie under my wraps. I like to think about my own ideas, and sometimes another thing pushes in, like now I remember I have to wash the crockery properly, it's been a while since I did it. I should also give the ice-box a proper clean with boiling water, we still have some caustic soda I think, I'm sure there'll be enough.

—

We're in the truck and Queenie's talking about people following us.

What makes you think that? I say.

I don't know, Win. It's a feeling is all. She says that I'm young, that I don't know what can happen in the world. That you have to be careful, always and everywhere.

I suppose someone could be following us but I don't really believe it. I try to remember the faces each day when we stop, and as we set up and tear down I look at all of them. If someone stands a while near the truck or pats Maude and gives her a carrot, or whenever we're at a rest stop or a CWA hall, I try to remember the faces but I haven't seen one reappear or anybody that makes me think they're interested in us. Not beyond what we might give to them or their children which is a few hours of entertainment, an escape from whatever their worries might be. People only care about what's going on in their own lives.

Tonight during the show I'll look at the crowd extra close. I say crowd but we know it won't be and you realise it too by now. I've never experienced what it is to perform in front of a large group and I wonder how that would be. Valentina says it lets you believe you're a giant even if it's only for the time of the performance. To be able to make a big audience laugh if that's what you want, or to cry if that's what you choose. How that would be, I can't imagine. Maybe with a bigger crowd that feeling would be made extra and I'll be honest with you, I would like to feel all of that even if it's only as a clown.

—

Queenie told me once she was performing and in the audience she counted fourteen women she'd reclaimed.

And their husbands sitting right beside them with no bloody idea, she said. Excuse my. You're sorry if a plant dies but in the end it's only a plant. All those years, I never had a one come and be cross or send a letter to say they wish they hadn't of. But all the women calling to say thank you, sending pictures of their lovely happy-borned children as if to say: See, I am a mother. See? I love these ones.

—

It's true that Queenie knows the things that happen in life in a way I can't. She knows that sometimes you can't control what happens to you. Once a woman came right up to her at a market and said, Are you the one who kills babies? We got out of there fast, Queenie was holding my arm so hard it left a mark. But then half an hour later and we're in a bakery and a lady comes up and hugs her and was saying thank you, she said it over and over. Queenie turned to me and said, See?

Later she said, Listen, Win, that first woman. She definitely never had one.

One what?

You know. Has never been in that situation. People who haven't, they don't understand and that includes the men of course. They've got no imagination and they've got no curiosity. They live in a world that lets them believe a reclamation is bad and wrong when really it's fine and necessary. Those women who like to judge, they'll have things wrong in their lives but they don't realise how lucky they are to never have a pregnancy they don't want to keep. If they need one or a daughter does, then they turn right around and get it done. Conservatives. Religious. Of course it's fine and necessary then. They get them too, of course they do, but it's all done in secret.

—

We go through places called Deepwater, Rollingstone, Blackmountain. The rivers are the Burdy, the Barron, the Tully. Wide flatlands formed by downfaults and lined with gypsum and salt. Some places have nature parks or kangaroo gardens or a heritage railway society, while others have a recycling centre or rabbit works. As we pass, Girl is against the window, she's talking about pineapples, occasionally turning to us with a smile, and I notice her hair needs a cut, the fringe is across her eyes. I'll have to trim it, she won't be able to see where she's going soon.

—

There's a highway patrol with the new brown uniforms, they're stopping us on the road. Valentina calls them fascists as she changes down the gears in the truck. She told me they're nothing but instruments for the state. She says they want protests filmed and their violence known because it will make people scared and easier to control. Their checks aren't for anything in particular, just the usual which is drugs, guns and money but they do it because they can, not because they must. Queenie says while some bad people do bad things because they must, most do it because they can.

One of the men puts his face in at the window and calls to Girl down the back, asks her if she wants to touch his badge but she says no. They come in the side, they look a long time at Queenie's hairdressing equipment, opening the case, lifting things out. When they hold up the rubber gloves she says, For dyeing, for perms and that. She has an answer for everything. They climb on the roof, up the ladder at the side, to check what we have stored there. They're confused by the description of the flat-packed structures, the automata, they don't understand what they're for.

Then they start to walk to the Mercedes which is where we keep the guns and the phone, they're in a secret place but even so. Valentina gets out to go with them and she pulls ahead, she's talking to them in a friendly way over her shoulder. The police slow their walking, they stare at the back of her at her bottom as she goes ahead, walking in a special way that is nothing close to clown. She goes to the driver's side and leans in at the engineer's window and says, How you going, big boy? And behind her come the police and now they're saying we have a broken tail-light but we know that's a lie, we never have a broken tail-light. The engineer is getting out now, she says she'll fix it, she always says that because we don't want any trouble. They go around the whole of the car, they're banging the sides all the way. Then they come back and that's when they say we can leave. The engineer's ears are still red as she gets back into the Merc and she pulls out and we pull out too and continue down the road.

I'M BY THE river, I'm by myself, my shoes are off and the sun is fully out, it's rare. On my body, all along it up and down, and I can smell something, there's a plant nearby. I don't know the name but it makes me remember sugar biscuits and how the engineer made them once we ate them hot off the pan, that was a long time ago.

The others are back at camp, I left them behind and I'm lying on the ground. I don't care about the dirt or that sticks might get in my hair. I'm here with Maude, she's standing nearby. I listen to the huffs she makes through her nose as she grazes the grass, how she shakes her head so her ears flap. It makes me think she's happy and hearing it makes me happy too. I should try to remember this moment. I should try to remember, hang on hang on, until the time the sun next comes out because it will happen, it will happen eventually.

—

I don't know what you would say but I've been thinking about it a lot lately. If the baby won't survive being born at twenty weeks then should that be the cut-off? What if the woman doesn't realise she's pregnant? When should the cut-off be?

ANOTHER DAY, THE last one, and this morning Queenie said rain so we're keeping an eye on the sky. We're wondering whether it will be big or small because even a quick shower can change a day or the evening. People, they don't want to come out in the night-time. We know that when it's wet they don't want to leave their houses or their camps no matter how much they might look forward to the show. Queenie keeps looking up as the sky thickens, the uncloud has a kind of shadow and the colour is coppery. You might think it strange depending where you're from but for us it's normal. The engineer said it won't be long driving to the next place and we're glad for that because the road will be slow if it does get wet. The big storms haven't come yet but they're on the way.

—

We're almost at the town now, we've been here a few times. There's a good cafe Queenie wants to visit and I told Girl there's a lolly shop nearby, that maybe we can look at the window if she likes. She's happy and says, Yes, please, Win. Queenie says, Don't buy her any mind, it's those teeth, and I say that we'll go for a look but first we have to drop in to the post office and leave a flyer and check the held mail because there might be a new booking or two before home.

—

Some of us go to the grocer and the rest of us to the post office. We pass stores with shoes and fabrics, and glassware. We stop a while in front, there are lots of pieces all of them vintage, and I say to Girl that Queenie has a collection of that, that it's called carnival glass. She got most of it from Nanango Show, she had a sister near there, I say, and I look into the window and there's Queenie's face in the reflection, it's a bit something-something. I can't say what she's thinking but I don't think it's about her collection of glass. Maybe it's about the other piece in her collection, the jar with her son inside. Queenie told me never to talk about it or what we do, not to anybody ever.

You want a nice husband one day, don't you? she said, and I couldn't say no 'cause I think I do, I really think I do.

Girl notices me looking around, she sees me stopping. Who are you looking for, Win? she asks, and I say no one and pinch her arm.

Come on, I say. Keep up.

She tells me not to be mean. Why are you so mean to me, Win? Why are you always so mean?

BACK IN THE truck, driving again and when we kill the lizard I'm not watching the road.

It was sitting in the middle, Girl says. It wasn't doing anything. She starts crying.

The engineer checks with Queenie. Should I pull over, boss?

No, keep going, she says. It's not safe here.

Girl is howling and I'm telling her to shush, that it'll be okay and not to be upset.

It didn't do anything to us, Girl says, and Queenie goes, Here, and makes Girl sit on her lap. Queenie's trying to console her, she's saying, Don't worry, there's lots of lizards in the world, but it isn't the right thing to tell Girl, it really isn't. Sometimes Queenie isn't very sensitive.

Did I tell you Cleopatra was once agisted with a farmer? Queenie says to Girl. That means staying there while we went on a small side tour. But she kept breaking out and coming to find us. Once she walked forty miles to catch up, all through the night. She walked everywhere with us if she wasn't in the semi, alongside the show or drifting off to the verges to find the tasty weeds, she liked to eat those best. Pearl and I ran alongside with little hand scythes to cut the sweet-greens for Cleo. She followed on her own, she never had to be tied up neither, and we only put her in the truck when we had a long jump or the roads were bad. She never disappeared, apart from one time when she took herself off for a holiday, it was for a week. We weren't sure where she went for all of that time but someone spotted her in the Dumaresq River, she was right in the middle with her trunk sticking out of the water, you couldn't see anything of the rest of her. She preferred to walk, she hated the trailer but if she had to go in she would. Oh, she was a good girl, she was the best.

She's trying to distract Girl but it makes her cry even harder because she wants animals, she wants to have elephants or lions. Even dogs would be good, she says, and Queenie tells her, There's a few differences between lions and dogs and Girl says, Yes, lions can kill you but dogs just love you no matter what.

In the truck I hold Girl's hand and say to her, Tell me what the lizard looked like, and she says, She was brown with yellow lines down her side and she had a long tail, and the more she describes the lizard the more she calms. She has her head down on Queenie's chest now and Queenie smiles and I smile back.

Girl is a good one we all like her a lot, but sometimes she cries too much and it never stops any time soon.

—

Later she's asleep and we talk about the lizard.

What happened? I ask. It was just a lizard on the road.

It's not about the lizard, Queenie says. It's about the person she misses most, who she wishes was on the road with a thumb stuck out asking to be picked up when we pass by.

I get it then and of course it makes me wonder whether anyone could be on the road for me one day, with their thumb stuck out.

Queenie sees what I'm thinking and she says, Don't be silly, Win. Nobody hitchhikes anymore.

—

Sometimes Girl gets on the truck radio at night. We told her never to say where she is or her name but she's allowed half an hour and she has to keep the door open, that's the rule.

Hello, she says. Is there anybody out there?

She goes through the channels and repeats her question.

Hello. Is there anybody out there? Hello?

—

Same day same tyre, the rim is acting up. It'll take a while the engineer calls back, says that we'll be here for a bit. We sit beside the road to wait and she fetches her tools and I ask if there's time to get the stove going and she says no, that it won't be that long. Queenie tells me to remember Dettol and pads. They're on the list, I say. We're all tired, we all want to be home we only have one more stop. I catch a view of Girl, she's walking on her hands down the road. There's no traffic in either direction of course and there hasn't been for two hours.

The Dettol reminds me of one time we got to a reclamation. After we emptied the uterus there was bleeding and when it came time to pack her, there was nothing so Queenie had to take off her slip and press it against the blood. She said it was as clean as anything else we'd be able to find and she didn't make a fuss in front of the woman but she never let me forget it either. It was my job to check everything was stocked, she said. After that I made sure there were plenty of towels all folded and put away and plenty of pads too.

They used to tell the customers to bring their own, Queenie says to me. Pads and towels. Now she's got her old memories going and she's waving her hand against her face because of the heat. Maybe we should be on the other side of the truck where it's cooler but we wouldn't be able to watch Girl, we like to keep an eye on her. I don't know how she can be on her hands on the road, it must burn them but she's tough like that, it's as if her skin doesn't have any nerves left in it.

We went through towels like you wouldn't believe, we asked the women to bring their own, but nowadays it's too risky to ask about towels, Queenie says. They notice anything you do different, husbands that is. People didn't use to care about what you did with towels. They simply didn't care.

Is that why you started the salon?

That's why we started the salon. A husband doesn't mind if his wife wants to look nice, maybe a permanent wave, a special updo. It's a reason to be carrying towels as well.

I look down the road, I can't see Girl's legs.

Where is she?

Over there.

I think there's something wrong with her.

Queenie says, What do you mean?

Be clear, she says. Be clear about what you mean. I say I'm not sure, that it's more a feeling than anything else. I think things have changed for her, I say. I think she wants something but I don't know what it is. I don't think she knows what it is.

Wants something? Queenie tips her head. Win, she says. I say that I can't explain it.

I walk away from her to where the engineer's feet are sticking out from under the truck and before I can ask how long she says, Not long now.

You always say that.

I go across the road to the fence.

I watch Girl on the road. Valentina told her she can start doing her own clown make-up next year, that she'll test her in a few more weeks. Until then she can only look at us doing it in the mirror and not even try it once herself, but if she's patient, Valentina will give her the box of paints to have a go.

You'll have to create your own, Valentina said. You can't use the face I've been putting on you, that's my face, you can't copy it.

Win? Girl said.

It's true, I said. You can't have her face and you can't have mine. A clown has to make their own face, it's always been that way.

Since then I've been finding small bits of paper with different designs, all of them with angry eyebrows and straight-line mouths. She's getting good at it but I don't want her to be an angry clown, even if she is the Whiteface. I want her to be a happy clown, I want her to be that.

—

The river has reeds lining the banks, they're tall and yellow-white, much like wheat down south-west. We haven't been there for years, we haven't been that far south, that is. There are bulrushes now too, Queenie calls them cattails. We used to talk about the plants we passed, sometimes I'd call out their descriptions and she would say, Yes, that's a cumbungi, or, That sounds like phragmite, but she isn't interested these days so I point out the ones I know. I point them out to Girl and she repeats the names.

Behind the reeds there's a wide channel of water, it looks deep but maybe it's not, they say it's hard to tell without checking. I say to the others that when I die I'd like to be wrapped in a white shroud and float down a river in a burning boat like a Viking and Queenie says, Don't you be talking like that, it gives me the chills.

We drive on. We're quiet until we pass through a town. Sometimes we move about the country in circles and this is a town we know, and now from the back, Girl counts what she's calling the broken houses. They have long grass and smashed windows and too many cars parked in front. Houses with dogs at fences and raised flags and sometimes there are painted signs if someone's selling cucumbers or tomatoes.

We pass the Bode place. Their dogs aren't behind a gate, they run out barking as we pass, and the windows of the house are covered with sheets. There's a line of cars in the driveway and outside on the road there are more, it's a gathering but not a party.

Because of the girl, Queenie says, she must have died, and I want to say she was Bip. I want to ask, Why don't you use her name? I've been thinking about her ever since. I think of those girls inside that house, behind the fence that's ruined and falling. Being there with that father, it must be a hard place to live, a hard place to be.

I know what you're thinking, Queenie says. You shouldn't. We were trying to help.

I don't say anything. It makes me sad to think of any girl in a wooden box with her life ended like that.

Stop to the side there, she calls up front. Win, take a new voucher, put it in the letterbox. So I do. FREE SHAVE. Standing outside I can hear the music.

We drive away, we pass other houses on the outskirts of town. Some have crosses drawn on the doors or fences, they're done with chalk or paint. We see bones hanging from looped strings on verandahs and on gates too.

What are they for? I ask, and while I expect Queenie to say, Nothing, or, I've no idea, it's Girl who says, They're for spells.

Queenie says spells aren't real, that they're only to scare men, and Girl says, Men can be witches too.

No they can't, Queenie says.

I don't know about witches. I haven't thought about them much to tell you the truth, but Girl has. She talks about how they move and how they laugh and what they do to small children either alone or in groups. I tell her witches aren't real and she looks as if she feels sorry for me.

I say again that witches aren't real and she says, Okay, Win, I believe you.

—

Later I ask Queenie about the crosses and she tells me that it means someone's pregnant, that it's a sign for the community. Neighbours asked to spy on each other and of course they do because sometimes there's a cash reward for people who go to the authorities. I don't ask her any more questions. I don't really want to know.

OUR FINAL STOP for the day and we're all glad. Girl comes out to where we're standing, we're in the middle of a sweep of pasture back from the river. She walks through the couch grass, there's a lilac tinge on the bunny tails and there's a breeze, it washes over the land, changing the colours as it goes. She's energised by the wind, she runs around to sweep the tails with her hands and stops to pick a bunch. Then she turns in circles looking at the sky.

She's here now, leaning against me and swiping her handful of plants along my arm.

What are you two talking about?

The clown opens her arms as if she's hearing a song and maybe it's Strauss or one of the show tunes we play on the hurdies. She says, Look. That is it. That is what there is and that is all there is.

You mean the bunny tails? Girl asks.

Those trees over there? I say.

Yes, Valentina says, both of those. But look at the sky. The sky's the thing for me.

I realise what she's saying. We see different things and in that moment what is in front of me is the white sun and wide grasslands. There's the wind, it's becoming a little stronger now, and as it grows it will make Queenie sick and carry dust into the Bedford and that will put us into a mood because we won't be able to keep it clean. For now though the wind is in the trees, over where they line the river. It's making them dance, the leaves round and silver.

Valentina says this is all that there is but I hope there is something more, something more for me. I want to know for myself, though. I want to find it for myself. I don't want to be told, I'm tired of being told. I want to see whatever it is for myself.

IT'S AFTER SUPPER, we had tomato and onions on toast and then peaches and cream which was nice, we haven't had cream for a long time. The vehicles are packed for tomorrow and we'll be home after the dentist. Girl's in my lap she's watching the fire with her weight against my chest and it's lovely. Even though she isn't mine I feel like she could be and while you might think it strange that a girl, which is myself, wants to pretend I have a child of my own, well there it is. I can only say what I have in my heart.

Listen, the clown says, and it's me she's talking to. I'm looking at Girl's hair, how the light from the fire illuminates her fringe. I trimmed it before dinner and I can see how crooked it is, that I've done a very bad job.

Win?

What? I say.

Things won't always be like this.

I nod because that's what she expects. We all know that being on the road is hard yet it's when we're sitting here in these times after dinner with our bellies so full that we're relaxed and numb, it's as if things might be okay after all.

—

Girl asks whether people used to get fed to the lions and Valentina explains the Roman times. How prisoners or soldiers were put in the ring to fight the animals, that it was a show and the audience liked to be scared.

I don't like to be scared, Girl says.

Like when Win is up high and the audience get excited. That's what I mean, Valentina says. Excited.

I still don't like it. I don't like it when Win's up high, Girl says. Then she remembers the dog.

I don't think the dog would like being up high either. She starts to cry.

When bad things happen to other people, it makes anyone watching feel better. Valentina's trying to explain this to Girl. That if death touches someone else, instead of being frightened we can be happy that we're being left alone. That what we feel is relief because it's passed on somewhere else. If someone dies in our presence surely it cannot come for us, not right then. It has to circle around and go elsewhere before coming back.

But Girl doesn't understand, she's too young. She's sad. She's sad for the dog and she's sad for herself.

The history of the triple somersault, Valentina's saying now, is a history of death. She's trying to change the subject because talking about lions eating people is too close but I wish she'd stop talking about all of it.

I remember when she told me about the triple. I was small like Girl and what it made me want to do was try it. For a long time I wanted to be the person who could do a triple, and although I didn't manage it maybe Girl will be first, maybe she'll be the one to get to do it first.

—

That night under my thick cover I think of the space station. They say NASA is supporting the ISS. They say that it's in low Earth orbit with five international agencies all of them with lots of letters in their names. There's the Lunar Gateway, which is going to be a communication hub, a science lab and a sleeping station for groups of agency astronauts and government people. But we think it's a secret project, no one trusts them to do anything right up there because why would they. We think the group were headed there, we think they've lost their way. Something's gone wrong and so every day we check if there's news but there's nothing on the billboards, there's nothing on the radio, nothing new at all. The talk of colonising Mars is old. The engineer says now it's all about tourism because people will pay big money to go and see whatever is there or to leave whatever is back here. She says maybe tourism's the wrong way to think of it. That maybe it's emigration. People going somewhere better to either die or start over again.

THE WOMAN

I LIKED MY nursing course but I had no friends, no real friends. That morning I'd broken up with my boyfriend, or he with me, I suppose. He hadn't come home and I'd waited all night crying. He was older and some might say that was part of the problem, others might say it was the whole of the problem. He arrived and took one look at my face and got his things. Told me I was being stupid. That I was being jealous and he wouldn't stand for it. He said he'd been clear from the start and I wasn't allowed to change the rules now. I tried to hold on and he became angry. He left our flat and I went to the bathroom to put water on my face. In the mirror I saw how it was beginning to swell.

Later that day, I saw the Reverend at the protest. How he stood, how he spread his legs as he held the bullhorn to his mouth, how he rocked on his feet up to his toes. I saw the energy in him, it was a power he later described to me as the might of righteousness. He saw me as well, he told me later. He saw me and knew that I was meant to go with him. It didn't take him long to persuade me. My face had not gone down but I went. Was it a mistake? Who can say anything much about their life choices until later? There's no perspective yet. You can't know it at the time, not until you've grown and moved past and can look back. That's when you might understand if a thing was bad or good. It's only then that you might understand what happened.

WIN

IT'S A STRANGE morning. Queenie says there's something odd when she smells the air but of course she can't say what, other than it's something burning. The clown takes a road off the highway, she's driving the Merc and we follow behind. We pass around the base of a hill where the trees are burned and there are white smoke wisps, they're coming off the ground. We all of us put up the windows but not before the smell comes in and that's when we go quiet. We see the huddled bodies of animals in the clearings, there's lots of them dead. Mounds that used to be wombat and koala, we see their blackened faces, their bared teeth. I tell Girl not to look and she climbs into the back and onto Queenie's lap. Up front the engineer tells me in a low voice about pictures she once saw, it was people dead from a bomb in another country. What she noticed was how they were lying, how they looked like they were asleep. Where they fell was where they stayed, they hadn't been collected up, they hadn't been made orderly for the photos. She was sorry for them, alone on the floor with no one who loved them nearby. It was the strongest feeling she had at that time, that they had no one there for them, that they had died alone.

ANOTHER TYRE ON the Bedford, the whole of it is shot away with shredded parts left on the road behind us. The tube is ruined so we put a new one in, but it's an inch shorter than the tyre, it's four instead of eight in the ply, and the rim on the wheel has worn down so we jam some washers in. We go another half-hour before the tyre is flat again and we have to change it completely. You should have seen how it was in the old days, says Queenie. Thirty vehicles, it was a wonder we got ten miles in one jump. Once we're going again, the engineer talks about the elephant semi. Remember? she asks and Queenie says, Of course. Driving that was a real ride. You'd go two feet forward then one back with the swaying of the elephants in the back. Oh, I got so seasick, it was terrible and you'd have to take a little brandy after.

I say that I'd like to drive an elephant semi.

It's not all that, Queenie says. As well as making you sick, we'd leave one town in the a.m. and sometimes not even reach the next until the following day.

I wouldn't care, I say. It would be something different.

—

We see a walking prayer group on the road. We pass them and their signs say SANCTUARY and KINDNESS but Queenie says those types are like any other, she says they're just not open. They're all misguided, they're all extreme. The engineer slows and the group crowds to the side to make way for us. They have small drums and there are children on men's shoulders. Then I see someone my age, it's a guy. I watch him and he smiles and tips his hat.

Well, that's old-fashioned, Queenie says. What a charmer.

But I'm not listening to her. I'm looking in the rear-view and he's bowing after the truck, he's lifting his hand in a wave. The group converges in the middle of the road and they continue their singing and clapping. I want to jump out but I sit and I stay and we drive on.

—

We're in the truck and the things are on the boil.

Nothing better than stainless steel, Queenie says. It cleans up very well.

I guess, I say. I don't know the names of them. When she gives me instructions it's Pass me scraper, Pass me pointy.

Sometimes I wonder how it would feel to have those things inside of you but she says it's best I never find out but that if I do, well that's life, that's fine. That women will forever want reclamations and others will forever fight against it but it's best we don't get involved in the back-and-forth of it.

Don't waste energy, don't waste words, she says. Action is always better.

She's waiting, she wants an answer.

I suppose so, is what I say.

—

We're there, it's me and Queenie and the engineer, but afterwards I don't remember much. I see it with my own eyes, you won't believe what I'm about to say, but it's true. We've finished our sandwiches and a woman arrives, she's early for her appointment and her belly is taut. She's near her time, I mean her birthing time, this is not a reclamation. She walks from her car to the truck and every few steps she has to stop and lean.

Late labour, Queenie says.

We get her inside, she won't let us do an internal but Queenie can tell how far she has to go which isn't very far, the baby is almost here. Queenie says to get a plastic bag one of the big ones, she says, so I go and get it.

This is the first time I see it and it will be the last. The baby comes out and before I can even look Queenie has put her back to me. She holds it by the ankles, she puts it in the bag, twists it to close and ties the top. She goes outside the annexe and behind me the woman is saying she doesn't want to see it, that she can't keep it she just can't have it. She doesn't give her reasons and Queenie never asks. Like I said, we never ask why, we give them what they want.

Queenie comes back and tells her to hush.

There are no judgements here, is what she says.

We wait until the woman has rested a while and then once she's paid and gone to her car and driven away, that's when Queenie tells me that sometimes we have to let the baby go. That's how she puts it but kill the baby is what she means. I say it's cruel and she says, No, Win, cruelty is what happens when you're left alone with something growing inside of you that you can't have. Cruelty is when they put a baby inside of you and force you to grow it in your body. When they make you keep it but you can't have it because you just can't.

None of it is right, I say, and that's when I start to cry. I'm upset she said 'we' because it wasn't me it was her.

She tells me to stop. That she won't talk any more about any of it.

Outside is the esky and the baby is in there. I want to help it, I'm thinking maybe I could have it. It's not until we're back with the others that Queenie continues the conversation that I thought was finished.

Listen to me, she says. How can I be for part of a thing and not the whole of it? One husband branded his wife with a hot iron and another, he cut into her—he cut into her leg with a knife then rubbed in ink to make a mark.

I say I don't believe it and she tells me that's my decision but that I can't actually choose whether something is true or not. It's how things work, she says.

It doesn't sound like things do work, I say, and she replies, Exactly.

I suppose after listening to all of this you'd think a person would let nature happen when they don't want to have it, and it's true that some people will do it that way. When they've made their final-final mind up they'll take it to a paddock and put it in the middle away from the road and leave it, sometimes they press the mouth and nose first. Queenie says I'm judgemental but all I can say is she has her ideas and I have mine. She says that there has to be something between good and bad and clever and stupid, and not because we want more categories but because we should be able to find ways to talk about all those points in between. If you think properly, she says, it's those bits in between where most of us live our lives, and I get what she means, I really do. But there's a but and that's what I'm thinking about. It's like the weather, there's just no middle anymore. We have storms or we have fire or wind or rain. Heat or cold, big wet or dry, but there's no spring, there's no spring at all.

—

I don't want to be Obelia. I don't want to learn a dental act. I don't want to ride a motorbike in a cage like Queenie wants and be called Winnstay the Flaming Cage Rider no matter what anyone says. She thinks people will pay more to see a girl doing it but what will it do to me? Once I start she won't let me stop and I'd have to be in that cage riding in circles until I die and sometimes I wish I was like Queenie at the time when she joined, it was simpler then. Practising flips on a bag of chaff or on one of the horse's backs going round and round the ring with a rope tied around her waist. The rope it went to a pulley system at the top of the tent so that when you fell someone had the end and they held you up, they called it a mechanic. It was to keep you from falling but we don't have them anymore because we don't use the tent, it's not practical. Not even Girl has a mechanic which means we do what we have to do without a rope, we just have to do it all on our own.

THIS IS ONE thing I know to be true. A person can be unclear about something and then a small part will shift and that's when understanding starts to leak in, like light in the morning at the edges of a curtain in a caravan. I begin to imagine that I could go somewhere new, away from the truck with its particular smells and sounds, the tap of metal against the dish and the sighs of Queenie as she does a hard one. Go away from the heaviness I feel when I see how big a woman is. Away from the gentle voice Queenie uses to give instructions once a customer's reclaimed and properly awake and starting to sit up with a pad between her legs. It's always me who has to help them down from the table to the recovery chair, where I give them a cup of tea if they wish, put rollers in, and they stay a while, they sit and stare at nothing but sometimes make jokes, sometimes laugh because that's normal too, the relief of it.

I don't really care about the reclamations. I think they're the right thing. But the truth is I don't want it to be me. It can be someone else, I just don't want it to be me.

I think and think about the cut-off because I don't know when that should be.

Queenie's walking this way, she has something to say, it's in her face.

It's a dispatch, she says. The Bodes are coming. The Bodes are coming and I want you to help because it's both of them. We have to do them both.

THE BODES ARE here and Mr is driving with Mrs sitting in the front passenger seat. When they get out, him fast and her slow, Queenie's moving, she's going to meet them. We're still alone, the clown and engineer aren't back from town, they went to get a new tube for the tyre and they took Girl with but Queenie doesn't seem surprised and I understand it's because she knew the Bodes were coming.

She's at their car and Mrs Bode is frightened but pretending to be angry and he is angry, there's no pretending there.

You've brought the voucher? Queenie is saying. It doesn't matter if you forgot. She's smiling at Mrs Bode. Never mind, we can still do the free shave. Win, get the towels.

I'm not here for a shave, Mr Bode is saying. We got your paper in the letterbox but we don't want anything from you. I'm here to find out what happened to my girl. She says it's your fault. She said you did something. Every time he says 'she', he jerks a finger at his wife.

Mrs Bode is shaking her head, she's shaking her head at Queenie and she's shaking it at me.

Let's sit, Queenie says. She takes Mrs Bode's elbow and escorts her into the annexe, she goes ahead so he has to follow, which he does because there's nothing else he can do.

Once we're there, Queenie sits them both down. She's very careful not to touch him.

We can set up quickly and talk while I'm doing it. Why not? Queenie's voice is fake but I'm the only one who knows it.

Mr Bode might be angry but he wants to show he's reasonable. Queenie said to me she's sure he listens to his daughters saying, Daddy don't but does it anyway and that if pressed, he would say that they provoke him. He's a man whose weakness comes from outside and it sets upon him in a rush but he would say it's a weakness that becomes manifest because his daughters are wicked otherwise he would never.

He lets Queenie put him in the chair. He lets her talk to him about making a cup of tea after and discussing whatever it is that concerns him. Let's talk about this, she says. But after a nice shave. He allows her to delay the moment of confrontation because in the end, in the deepest part of him, he doesn't want to face his place in this, not even secretly. He allows her to tie a towel around his neck, and Mrs Bode sits in the chair next to him.

How about a quick refresh for you? Queenie says to Mrs Bode. Those curls could do with a spruce. Mrs Bode doesn't reply which Queenie takes as assent. Let's give you a tidy, she says. Just the front and top is all you need.

I heat the towel for him and tie a cape around her. I start with a bit of a scalp massage and Mrs Bode closes her eyes. When Mr Bode is reclining with the towel wrapped around his face, he starts to speak. He says he told the minister about us and that's when Queenie takes the straight blade. She draws it across his throat then passes it to me. I shake my head so she pushes me out of the way and does the same to Mrs Bode. I want to make it sound as if they didn't struggle and went still straight away but they did struggle. We each had to hold them and it got messy.

We wait until the blood has slowed, we catch it in towels but there's a lot even so. Queenie won't look at me. She knows this is wrong and I do too but she says it's best for the girls, she says now they're free.

—

When the others come back we're sitting out the front. I take Girl for a walk. She's telling me there might be a good night for stars soon, that Valentina told her we could try to look. We leave so the engineer can deal with the Bodes. It will be too much for Pet to eat at one time so some of them will go into the gas freezer. It doesn't take the engineer long to cut up a body with a knife, maybe twenty minutes, but with two she'd use the axe and get it done in fifteen. Don't ask me how I know that, I realise it's not something a person like me should have in their head. Queenie says she's making the world a safer place but it seems as soon as one dies another one rises, born or made, so how can the world ever finish all of its badness?

Later I will ask her about Mrs Bode, about why we had to do her as well.

She was a helpmate, Queenie will say. You know that. She let it happen and that means she's as bad as him. Those girls will be free now.

I will tell Queenie that I do know but inside I don't, not really. All I have in my head now is that the girls don't have their mother. In my mind are more questions. Who will look after them? Will they be alright? Those girls in that house, will they be alright?

THE HEAD OF the secret police, Yezhov, visits the noted genetic scientist Lysenko. The scientist explains that they're having problems with the latest impossible task set by Stalin, which is to mutate the genes of a rabbit and change it into an elephant.

Yezhov boasts that the NKVD has the best scientists in the world. 'Give me the rabbit,' he says, 'and our scientists will solve the problem.'

A month later, Lysenko goes to see Yezhov in the Lubyanka. 'How is it going?' he asks.

'The job is done,' says Yezhov. 'One hundred per cent success. We have turned the rabbit into an elephant.'

'This I have to see,' says Lysenko.

So Yezhov leads him to a vast cavernous dungeon, large enough to hold a whole herd of elephants. In the gloom, some distance away, Lysenko can just about make out a tiny white creature. It is the same rabbit, holding his head and screaming, 'I'm an elephant! I'm an elephant!' (3 hours 45 minutes)

I'D LIKE SOMEONE to listen, I'd like to be able to speak but I think mostly what I want is to tell someone about the reclamations and how it feels to be a part of someone's hurt and someone's help at the same time. What it's like to be met at the door of a caravan by an old woman with blood up to her elbows. What it feels like to know a thing is necessary but still to hate it all the same.

—

This is another thing I know is true. You can't be a bit dead and you can't be a bit pregnant but you can be a bit good or a bit bad. If this isn't true, how can it be that people get up and testify to a man's good character when he's done awful things? Are they lying? Maybe it's camouflage, maybe that man builds testimonials early and only shows his true bad to the weakest, but even if Hitler was a good dog owner and Stalin a good father, that's not enough to cancel out the rest of what they were, not even close. It's not enough to be a little bit good, or only good to some people. You have to be good to everyone who deserves it all of the time and even to some of the people you think don't deserve it, even to them as well. You have to be good for being good because it's the right thing to do. No one is perfect, no one can be good all the time. But you have to try.

—

I go to Queenie and say that I want to stop. I don't want to keep doing it, I tell her.

What do you mean? You have to continue, she says.

I can't.

Of course you can, it's what you do. Why have I bothered with all of it for so long if not for you to go on? And next the girl will help. She'll be the one to help you.

Then I get it. I feel stupid because I didn't realise it sooner.

No, I say. Not Girl.

Yes Girl. Why else did we get her from the road? What's that face? I swear, Winnstay, you're dim sometimes.

I say maybe I want to get married. Maybe I want a husband.

No. No boys, none of that. She puts a hand to her chest. Especially not a fancy one, if that's what you're thinking.

I saw him at the show that night, his hair parted on the side with his lace-up shoes, and I saw that one on the road too, with his smart hat. You think those women who come weren't once like you? They had love and look what happened to them. We think we'll be different, that it'll be alright for us.

She's right. It is what I believe, that I'll be different.

You'll have to keep running the appointments when I'm not around, who else can do it? And Girl will help you.

I don't care who does it, I say. I tell her I want to be a normal person and that's when she turns mean. What man would want you, with what you've done? she says. You'd have to tell him. You can't keep something like that from a partner. Someone would tell him, he'd find out and it would make him hate you, make him leave.

Don't do it to Girl, I say but Queenie smiles. I'm sorry, love.

I walk away from her then. I get up and go all the way around the river. She's calling behind me, saying not to go far, that we need to take Girl to the dentist, that we have to get back to Arcadia, but I don't stop, I don't listen. I want to get as far from our camp, as far away from Queenie as I can.

THE WOMAN

SOMETIMES WHEN HE rests I can take myself away and find a spot behind the trees or over a rise where I put myself down to the earth. I take my time in the selection of place and sometimes there's not much choice, sometimes it's a dry terrain with dirt and sticks but no mind, I make do. Then off comes my fabric, a ritual of unpinning and unwinding, and I put it to the side and touch my head, prickled and sharp. I scratch and I like its feel, it wakens my fingers. I lie back, I stretch out my limbs, I'm on the ground and the earth holds me.

This is when I can think my purest thoughts without interruption, a meditation I cannot manage when driving or cooking or sweeping the tent. Today it's the dog. It's up there passing all of us by. And the others, the humans. Are there long-stringed arguments where they try to decide on a particular question, such as what has happened to them, what is causing their demise? Are others of them saying, Let's not waste our air, let's not use it up? Are they preoccupied with oxygen or with fire, or do they sit in a circle and let the love come, speaking words of comfort? Do they hold one another?

A story now, long forgotten but the astronauts have made me think of it. A hot-air balloon that fell to Earth for almost a minute and how the tourists all died, as well as the balloonist. They held one another as they fell and were found on the ground, arms linked in the basket, strangers knotted together.

I think of our dog, the one we had when I was a girl. How she rested her nose on anyone's knee, anyone who sat still. How she wanted to be with us, scooted herself in close. How we were her everything.

WIN

THERE'S A BAPTISM along the river.

The man is saying that Jesus was baptised by John in the Jordan. And that when he came out of the water immediately the heavens opened and the Spirit descended upon him, like a light it was, and a voice came from the sky: 'Thou are my beloved Son, with thee I am well pleased.'

He takes a woman by the back of her neck. She holds his wrist with her two hands and he ducks her all the way under, everything goes beneath the water.

We put that old life behind us, we step forward in Christ, he says.

When she comes up, she falls into his outstretched arm and his other hand is at her neck. She puts her hands up in the air.

Next is a girl and the Reverend does the same to her.

Are you ready to walk with Christ?

Yes, sir.

Are you willing to give your life over?

Yes, sir.

He prays over her head before he puts her under but this time he holds her nose.

Out with the old stuff, he says as he ducks them over and over, all the people, and as they rise, he says, Come on into the love. And all of them, as they rise from the water, they put their hands up afterwards as if they've won a prize. They pull their wet shirts away from their breasts, that's the women, and away from their stomachs, that's the men.

The last person to get dunked is the guy from the show, the one with the manly forehead. As his head goes back his skin shines pale blue under the water, and once he's up his hair drips and his friends cheer from the banks. I stand there. I can see his nipples sitting dark under his shirt.

The preacher finishes and I realise it's the same one, the man who came to our camp, the one from the road. I look around and up on a small rise, there's the woman, there she is with her white headdress. I hope she doesn't see me.

I have to get back, I go the way I came and pass by the guy and to be honest, I decide to walk that way it wasn't an accident. His face is open, he's happy after hearing what a girl has said to him, she said it right into his ear just now. I smile at him I want him to notice me but what it brings to his face, what shows there on his mouth, well it's a wince, I can't describe it better than that. I know then how ugly I am. I feel beyond stupid. Why did I smile? I'm so ashamed.

—

At camp, Queenie is waiting because we need to leave for the dentist. We say goodbye to the others, that we'll see them at Arcadia in the evening, and then it's her and me and Girl, we get in the Merc and we leave.

Girl is at the window, calling out the things she can see. I hope she won't need to have any teeth taken out and I hope we can get it done quickly, I want to leave this area. Queenie opens a packet of biscuits and shares it around, and I keep my eyes on the road, putting my hand out when I'm ready for the next one. The biscuits are good, they're nice and sweet.

How's your mouth? I ask Girl and she says it hurts. Then it's lucky we're going to the dentist, I say, she'll fix you up, and Girl says she supposes so but she's not convinced, I can tell.

Then I'm looking for the turn-off. Queenie's told me it's set back off the road, hidden by the rise of a hill and a spread of ficuses, and she tells Girl about the dentist, it's on a boat, it's a paddle steamer painted grey, called the *Lady Sybil*. Queenie says they can anchor it in different places, it's been going thirty years or more. It's a good idea, a dentist that can move. Girl's never been, not even before is what she told us, which is not surprising. We know it's expensive, we know people let their teeth go until there's something really wrong. Then they visit someone who might have a poking tool or a digging tool, sometimes it's a pair of pliers that can take out anything rotted. But Margaret on the boat, she's gentle, she's good. She has a numbing cream or injection if she needs to hurt you and then it's not too bad, not at all, Queenie tells Girl. Sometimes she tells her captain to stop in this place or that to pick women up for a reclamation, Queenie says to me, and that's how I learn the dentist works at both ends.

—

We're driving and the road is one long curve. It's late morning, we've been going an hour and stopped once for Girl to go to the toilet, did I say she always needs to go? Queenie's singing a song, it's about a small boy who's travelling to Paris, and I think to myself I'd like to go to Paris, it's meant to be lovely and people say that they still have a spring. They say you can hold hands and sometimes there's kissing, that's what Valentina told me anyway.

I'm going to get there somehow. To see the people kissing in Paris.

—

Queenie's asleep. Tell me if you're tired, is what she says when I drive, and she lets me know she can take over but she sleeps now when we're in the car and her eyes are no good. She has her jar in its bag in her lap, her mouth is open her chin down, but I've got the map and on it the dentist is a red cross Queenie marked, it's up a track.

Sometimes, I'd like to pull over because being on the road so much makes me feel like we're flying in space, especially at night when the white lines float above the black of the tarmac and trees rise up at us in a rush at the side of the road. It becomes like a dream and I have to keep the speed down otherwise I can go into a trance and my foot starts to press down and I scare myself. I need to remember to be careful, that it's not a highwire and it's not the dive scaffolding. This is a more dangerous thing.

—

The final nine kilometres take longer than you would think but the track loses its surface, it becomes gravel then sand. We leave the forest behind and drive down a narrow road hemmed by trees. I catch sight of the river, it shows blue through the branches. I'm driving slowly and the melaleuca is bleeding sap but here now, we're out of the dark, we're in the wide open with the pastures of green and a big sky too.

The river is pushing along in the distance and I'm concentrating hard. The wheel jumps in my hands because of the rough surface, and beside me now Queenie is awake. We reach another sharp turn in the road and there's a small gate.

Go on, Queenie says, drive through, and we go a bit further, then come to a shack on the river bank, it's made of cement and I can see holes where the sheets have been spackled together. In the car park is a motorbike, one of those big ones with long handles, and there's a tail, it's an animal one tied to the backrest, maybe it's fox I can't be sure. The door in the shack opens, the dentist is coming out to meet us, she has someone with her which is a man with a gun.

Help me with the door, Queenie says, so I get out and go around to her side and next thing they're at the car.

Bethy, the woman is saying, and now we're moving away from the car and she and Queenie are hugging and Queenie's saying, Girls, this is Margie, and the man asks for the keys and Queenie says, Give them, Win, so I do. He goes to check the car, he does the inside and the boot, and he gets down on the ground and wriggles under with his gun beside him. Queenie and the woman have stopped hugging and Queenie is touching my arm and saying, This is our Win, and I say, Hello.

The waiting room is cold but I sit there while Queenie and Girl go on the boat. It stays at the dock, they only take it out to do reclamations, not to drill or pull teeth. In the room with me is a man, he's a patient, it must be his motorbike out there. I pretend to look at my hands, they're on my lap and then I get a magazine but I'm watching him all the same. His leather vest and bare arms with tattoos up and down, also his jeans and boots, all dirty. I can't see his face, not properly, until he lifts his head and there it is, a big moustache and hard eyes that swing across to look at me.

The magazine has an old story about the astronauts, how things were before they left with everyone happy, everyone looking forward to the launch. They were excited they said, all twelve of them. They'd done the training and were going to say goodbye to their families in another two weeks and then get strapped into the space shuttle to be blasted away from Earth.

When the others come back, Girl's holding her cheek. She's unhappy, I see it straight away, and she perches on the seat beside me, away from the man. She leans into me and asks, Who's that? I say that it's a waiting room so people wait here. Her face is closed.

Queenie comes over. Just the two rotten ones for now, Margie's taken them out, she says. Let's go have lunch at that place back on the highway, the roadhouse.

I drive us away from the river, away from that room with its old magazines.

How was it? I ask Girl. She's slumped against the seat so I angle the rear-view to be able to see all of her.

My tummy hurts, she says, my mouth hurts too.

As we pass along the rutted road Girl says, Ow, with each bump so I try to slow down but Queenie says, no that'll be worse. Go faster, she can't feel anything, she got numbed up good and she's just imagining it.

—

The roadhouse is for trucks mainly but there's one car, it's a sedan, and around it a family, maybe on holiday or maybe just to move, they might be leaving a bad place or going to one, who can tell. The menu has sandwiches and pies and of course Girl wants a cheese sandwich and I'll have a ham one and Queenie wants ham as well.

Go and give the order, Win. See what drinks they have. If they'll let us use the bathroom.

We're sitting there when the man arrives on his motorbike. I don't notice him but Queenie says, Wasn't he back at the dentist? And Girl says, Yes.

He doesn't look our way when he comes in, he goes straight to the counter.

Are we ready to leave? Queenie's picking up her bag and wrapping Girl's sandwich but first we need to go to the toilet, Girl says she needs to go.

Go with her, Queenie tells me, so I do, and all the time she sits on the toilet it doesn't sound like anything is happening.

Is it coming?

It's stuck.

We need to leave, you can try again later.

But my stomach hurts.

I lean against the basin.

She flushes and opens the door and washes her hands. We go back to Queenie, who's still sitting in the booth. She's watching the man who's outside near his bike, he's finishing a meat pie.

—

We drive half an hour and then we approach a car, it's a Ford coming towards us and as it gets closer I see the driver. It's a person wearing white up around their head and I recognise it's her and Queenie sees her too, the man sitting beside her, they pass in a flash. We're nearing a bridge, it's narrow and old, and when Queenie says to pull in right before it, I do. I feel it this time. They're coming for us.

There's a clearing on this side of the bridge but she says, Go further in. Go behind those trees.

I steer the car in as far as I can and park in the scrub. I don't like the way the trees are bending in the wind. I say to Queenie, Why don't you sit in the car? I'll have a look. But she says no, she's getting out with me, so what can I do?

Queenie tells Girl to stay and we open our doors. Out of the car it's cold, there's been a quick change and the wind is blowing fierce. Even so I can smell petrol, there must be a truck just passed on the road but I can't hear anything over the wind.

We wait but no one comes so we get back in the car. Girl is lying on the back seat with her eyes closed and we two sit, we don't speak. I imagine that the darkness of the car blends into the trees, and with the earth and hills spreading purple behind us I don't think we're visible from the road.

Queenie says we have to be careful when we have Girl with us.

If you're so worried, why are we sitting here? I ask.

We have to be careful of her, she says again.

What about me? I want to say. Don't you ever worry about me?

I ask Queenie, Shall we go? but then I see something, it's a car.

There's someone coming, I say.

What's that?

It's a car. Wait here.

I get the rifle from the boot and the pouch of bullets and I can hear the car is nearer now so I go behind a tree. It's the best one I can find, a wide gum.

I see the car, it's moving along the road, not too fast.

It's them.

They pull in and climb out and I try to tell myself not to be suspicious right away, that maybe they aren't here to hurt us. I'm thinking to leave the gun and try to talk but the man is shouting, KILLER.

I hope Queenie will stay hidden, maybe I can say something that will make them leave. I can tell them a story, so I step out from behind the tree but from the side I see Queenie walking towards them, she's moving fast for someone so old. I don't have a plan but I have to get over there, I have to be near Queenie when they meet but she gets to them before I do, she has her cane in one hand and the razor in the other.

I will cut you, she says to him.

And I will squeeze the life from out of you, he says. So it's true. You're the one killing babies.

Define babies, Queenie says.

And the men? Is that you as well? You think to play God?

Someone has to, she says. Where is he? All I know is he's not here. There's a wildness in her that I've never seen.

She looks at me. I'm not angry, Win, she says. I don't want you to think I'd ever be angry with you.

She raises her stick and brings it down on the woman's head. Crack it goes and the woman falls, and Queenie leans over and hits her again, she does it once more she's that fast, but then the man grabs her hand, he twists the cane from her fingers, bends her wrist to make her drop it. I hear a snap, the bone is surely broken.

Wait, I say. Wait.

I have the gun up, I pull the trigger, but there's no bullet in it of course, we keep it empty.

The man is punching Queenie in the chest and now he's on top, he's straddling her and has his hands around her throat. I run to them and put the muzzle on his back, I push at him from behind but he's strong, he won't get off, he won't stop what he's doing. I can hear his breath, he's making a strange huffing noise. The woman to the side, she's starting to stir, she's touching her head so I get a bullet and crack it into the gun. She's getting to her knees now, there's blood down her face and her white headscarf has slipped. Her head is bald, she has no hair. My gun is ready but she's on me now, she grabs the barrel, tries to pull it away from me. I have it tight in my hands, my finger reaches the trigger and that's when I shoot and she falls back.

I need to do the bolt again and my hands are shaking and I'm weak, it's that hard to slide it forward but I manage. I get the bolt pulled back and around but she's still down. I think maybe she's fainted and my finger is on the trigger and I go to where Queenie is with the man. He's still on her and I think it's been too long. His back is to me and he's talking to her, he's saying words but I can't hear them.

I get a bit closer, I touch the end of the gun to the back of his head. Let her go, I say.

I can't see Queenie's face but I can see her side, her shirt has ridden up and on her skin, at her waist, there's a mark, an old carving, one I haven't seen before, the ink black and blurred.

Let her go, I say again, but he doesn't stop. Now I can hear what he's saying. Here you are. Here you are.

Then I shoot him in the back of the head and he falls down and to the side and a lot of blood hits the ground. I drop the rifle to pull him off her, it's hard because he's tall and he's dead but so is Queenie, he's squeezed the life out of her. When I lift the top part of her body her head falls back, maybe he's broken her neck. I don't cry, it's all been too quick, she was alive and now she's gone. I pull her as far away as I can then sit down and that's when I start to cry.

—

After a while I lay her down and I go to the car but Girl's not there. I call out but she doesn't answer and this makes me scared. I have to get out of here. I get Queenie to the car, it takes a while. I push her across the back seat and put the blanket on top to cover her.

Girl? I call. She might be in the front on the floor, there but there's no noise from her.

I call again, outside the car.

The woman is trying to sit up now, so I get in the front seat, I start the car and drive out of the clearing.

My last view is of the woman, she's sitting up against the tree and she has one hand touching her head, the other lying in her lap. There's blood on her shoulder and that's the last thing I see of her before we turn a bend, then the car meets the sealed road and I drive.

—

It's raining. I don't know how long I've been here, a while I think. We're a few kilometres down the road, I wanted to get away from the bridge and I don't know how it's happened but time has passed. I remember hearing a whoop of something but I can't think how long ago it was and I've been sitting here in the car with Queenie in the back and in the lost time there's been other noises. The sound of rain on the roof of the car and windscreen, and movement on the road, noises loud and elongated.

I remember I don't have the rifle and I don't have Girl either. I need to go back. How I could have left her I don't know. I tell myself it's something that took over my body, that I didn't have a choice, it was automatic. Somehow the sun is starting to go down, which means it's been that long and soon it will be dark. Queenie thought I told them. She thought I told them where to find us. I imagine telling Queenie I'm sorry about Girl and I can hear her saying, Don't worry about it, duffer, and thinking about all of it makes me feel even worse.

Soon I'm back at the place and I can see the dark heap of the preacher's body by the acacia tree and there are puddles of water on the ground. On the other side is the woman, her head material is off, she's wrapped it on her shoulder.

I get out and look for the rifle but it's not there.

Are you alright? I say.

She says she is. It didn't go in, she tells me.

I ask about the rifle, I ask where it is.

It's not here. A man came and took it.

I don't understand what she's saying.

I help her up, she has her tambourine tied onto her belt and it rattles as she moves. Sit in the car if you like, I tell her.

The rain isn't stopping any time soon so I leave the car but I take the keys, I leave her and Queenie and walk in the other direction away from the road. The air is still, there's no wind now and I'm getting cold but still I call. I walk and I walk, I keep an eye to both sides. I'm hoping to see a head peeking from behind a bush, she'll want to see that I'm alone before she comes out. There's no pathway, not now, there's nothing to mark the way a person could proceed, and in the distance the ridge looms at the top with a small peak to the right, it's the colour of charcoal. The ridge is what brings rain to this place, they say.

Maybe she went the other way, it would make sense for her to have crossed the road and gone north instead. It makes good sense to go away from the bodies, to keep going the way we were headed. I'll walk a while longer in this direction then go back and do the same on the other side because it's the only thing I can think to do.

—

I told you when we found Girl she was very dirty but she let me help her wash that first time, she said I could, so I ran a bath in the tub out the back and she got in, she sat deep to her neck. I said I needed to wash her, that I'd use a cloth and was it okay if I touched her and she stood up for me. I think she let me because I was also a kid and I was gentle with her and I didn't say anything when I saw her buttocks, how they were scabbed, and how her back and thighs had marks as if she'd slept in thorn bushes.

And while overall she was small and hunched with her hands across her chest, I felt by the way her eyes never left my face that she was thankful. I asked her to lift her arms so I could get into the pits and I swept the flannel along her flanks and told her to sit down, that the water would wash the other bits. She sat and it made a splash and she looked at me quick like she was scared but I laughed, and I put my hand in the tub and squeezed it in a way that squirted water at her to show that it was alright.

Like I said, it was a long time before we got her hair right. Like I said, Queenie couldn't even come close with the scissors and I've been able to do her fringe only recently, but before that she would jump up, she would run if anyone came near with them, she'd run inside if we were outside or out to the garden if we were inside, and for me it was her face in those moments of running that made me sorry for her.

It was like she'd seen a monster but now I'm not worried about that, not anymore. What I'm worried about is that a monster has seen her.

—

We stay at the clearing, we sit in our wet clothes. The woman is beside me in the car, she doesn't complain, doesn't say she's cold. I ask again about her shoulder and she says it's not bad but that she's a fainter. Not good for a nurse, she smiles. What about your head? I ask and she says it's sore but fine. We don't talk beyond that and I realise that I'm not afraid of her, that there's no harm here for me.

Another big wind comes, it blows the rain away, and when the haze shifts around four a.m. I see the moon, I don't count the seconds but I guess it's thirty or forty big roosters. It's the first time I've seen it properly and Saturn and Jupiter are there too. How do I know it's them? you're wondering, well I don't, but I've decided that's what I think. I see stars, more of them the longer I look, and I hope that Girl is seeing them too, I hope she can see the sky.

The woman is asleep now. I keep awake but Girl never shows. We stay a few more hours into the morning and even some after that but she doesn't appear. We have to leave, I have to take Queenie home. I'll do that and then come back with the others. We can't go to the police. We can't do that.

—

I drive away from the clearing. I'm thinking about how the world is wide and wild and how it will be when it all ends. Some of the wideness is about the plains, they're up near the Darling, with all the kilometres of brigalow growing dense and high, and the sweeping vast stretches of the herb lands. The sky so broad with its smudged colours, and not forgetting the sea which we're near now, how it stretches to the horizon, grey or almost-blue, sometimes it can be both.

You might think wildness rests in animals only, well that's not the case. Mostly the wildness lives in humans, that's what I'm beginning to see. Beside me the woman sits, there's a bruise on her right cheek, it's mottled to brown. She was wild during the fight but now as she rests with her eyes closed, I see what she might have looked like as a child.

JOY

SHE'S A GOOD person letting me be along like this. We don't talk as she drives. I'm being taken somewhere again and it's a feeling I like very much. There's a beach a short way to the east and we go there. We sit on the old dunes, they're mostly gone now.

What are you going to do? she asks me.

Grow my hair.

Do you want this? She pulls a lipstick out of her pocket.

I take it.

It's Coral Blush, she points.

Oh, thank you.

She walks down the beach. There's a seagull on the sand. The haze hangs over the water. I see a broken pier in the distance and, above, more orange in the sky. It reminds me of a lozenge

I had once when I was little, when my throat was sore. Someone gave it to me to make me feel better.

She cries a bit longer then sits beside me. She asks me what my name is.

Joy, I tell her. My name was Joy.

WIN

THERE WAS A spacecraft called *BepiColombo.* It was sent to Mercury to gather data and it couldn't fly straight to the planet because the sun's gravity would pull it in. They had to make it go slowly, it did lots of laps but each time came a bit closer. This took years, but the thing is it couldn't go straight there, it had to go another way which is why I'm thinking about it instead of Girl. And after Girl, in another orbit is Queenie who I also can't think about. I couldn't explain if I tried, it just came into my head. I have to let my thoughts pass by them, I can't go straight there yet.

—

But I do think about the sisters. I keep imagining them in the house, the dogs barking outside, men knocking on the front door, they're knocking on the back door, looking through the windows.

Sitting on the beach Joy does the kindest thing. She takes my hand and studies the lines on my palm, she's wiping her thumb along them. She tells me everything will be alright. That my future will be happy, that I will fall in love and have children if that's a thing I want. After that, she holds my hand for a moment before she places it back on my knee.

You'll be okay, she says. She lifts and shakes her tambourine. She smiles at me and I see that she has one gold tooth.

—

The man took Girl. Maybe she'll get away so I'll come back and keep searching but for now we have to get home. The beach is behind us and we've gone an hour when the road ahead starts to shimmer. My eyes are gritty so I pull the car onto the verge to rest. We have to find a doctor for Joy, I suppose we could go to the dentist, she would know what to do. She might give me the name of the man. That's what we'll do, we'll go there but I need the engineer with me and maybe Valentina too.

Here the sky is an even stranger colour, like brown paint mixed with water, and the haze is definitely thinner, it's lifted or been blown apart by the wind. Maybe it is asteroid dust, leaked and come to settle on our planet. All the bad metals drawn here through the universe, brought like bad things that come to us eventually, that come to live in us and make us human.

—

We go past a dam and a petrol station. Then it's a sports oval with stadium seating outside a town, then a roadside stall, it has potatoes and horse manure. A petrol station where I fill up. I reach across to the glove box for Queenie's purse and I see the bag on the floor, it's her jar. I go and pay and then use the bathroom and Joy is in there, she's washing parts of her body at the sink. I use the toilet and then we keep going.

—

The road is long and narrow, it runs north and south straight as anything. You could take your hands off the wheel and the car would keep its course but I don't do that because I have Queenie with me and I have her jar and now there's Joy as well. I have to get back to the others, I have to tell them about Girl. That's what's important.

We drive and we drive and I see it in front of us, a wall of dust that reaches hundreds of metres into the sky, maybe a thousand. It hangs circular with bands of grey and white. It's creeping towards us, spreading and covering everything. Do I go through or stop?

I pull over and stop, I put the headlights on in case and we sit and we wait until the dust cloud arrives. It engulfs the car and outside all turns dark.

I'm trying not to fall asleep I'm that tired. I look out into it and on the plain in the swirling dim is a creature. It's tall and spindly with a long-legged, swaying gait. Small head and mottled skin that isn't really skin, and a tail dangling and tufted at the end. Then there's another, it's the elephant. There's someone inside, they're pulling levers and turning dials and the beast shambles behind the other. And now comes the lion, she's crouched low to the ground but I can't see anyone inside, it's too far away. The figures are moving but they're not going anywhere they have no reason, and I sit in the car and my eyes are open but truthfully I'm small and I'm helpless. Joy is looking at me.

I want to tell you something, she says. Let me tell you a story. It's real but feels like a dream to me. There was a truck. It was filled with people, they were sitting and holding their small possessions and after I'd looked at all the people, I made out that in the corner sat three old women, all tied by the neck. With a rope they were bound together and it was knotted so tight that their throats bulged. They were crying and calling out, hoping for someone to notice them.

A man came. He had a thick black marker, he put his initials on one of the women, scribbled on her cheek and passed on. Other women were there, they were younger, and they worked with small knives and nail scissors, they were trying to cut the old women free. They were good people, good strangers, trying to help.

What happened?

I don't know, we drove on.

Were you with him then?

Yes, I was.

Was he bad to you?

I don't know how to answer you, she says. I don't know what to say about that. She turns to look out the window.

—

Comedy and tragedy work almost the same because they both rely on a moment when a person passes from not knowing to knowing. This is called anagnorisis, Valentina told me. It's when the audience realises what has happened to the egg or umbrella or chair, or the double meaning of the words. It's this splitting of time when things can be funny or the opposite which leaves us laughing or crying for the rest of our lives, the best is both. The top clown gags are flexes in a world that just is because it's how the world is for everyone, with no resolution, no conclusions. All of it makes me want to laugh because now I realise what's happened: I have become full clown. Valentina said it would happen one day and I know that from this point onwards I will see the world through clown eyes. I will walk through the world with clown shoes and, like she's always said to me, this is not a bad thing. For some of us, it's the only thing we've got.

—

A clown sees something small and trivial but they don't walk past. When the clown stops and bends down to pick up the matchbox and accidentally kicks it across the stage and is unable to ever reach it, that's what's both funny and tragic. She's trying her best but failing, but you're not laughing at her. What you're doing is laughing because you understand what that feels like and you're sorry this person is having a hard time. You know it could easily be you but it's her right now and you laugh in that moment of recognition and shared humanity. The laughter is a kind of love.

Let's have intensity in the world. You come upon a flower, well it's a weed, one of those that grows alongside country roads or even footpaths in the cities. It's a small yellow one that someone has put in a vase, perhaps a child insisted, and you respond with rapture and with exaggerated movements of hands to face and joyful mouth and eyes wide open, extreme. You approach someone else to tell them about that flower, and you might think what's the point of it all but this is what's true about the world and each time the answer has to be *why not*? We clowns are in a state of radical empathy with the world. This is the greatest thing a clown can do for anybody or anything. Be open and be tender. Be ready to love because that's all you can do for another person, let alone yourself.

—

I've been dozing, the dust cloud has passed and I decide it was a dream. Outside is dusk, the land falling dark and shadows lengthening. I start the car and concentrate on the road because it's what I have to do. I'm thinking what next when there ahead in the middle of the road is a figure. It's someone lying down or maybe it's a pile of dark clothes, maybe a pile of rubbish I can't tell. I stop the car and to the sides are paddocks, the grass long and upright, and there's a flash of disappearing rabbit.

Do I turn around? Do I go back? What does my kind of clown do?

I can take the long way though it will add an hour. The others are waiting for us, they'll be worried because it's been a night but it can wait a little longer. I have bad news, who's ever in a rush to deliver the bad?

I get out of the car and as soon as I'm out it's like there's a kind of pressure, as if something large and heavy is a short way down the road, something that recognises me. It's coming closer, it's around me now, the air vibrates and I know what you're thinking, that it's a UFO but it's not that. It's something alive, a vast energy I can feel. I can't see it but if I reached out

I could touch it and it knows I'm there. I'm scared but into my head comes Queenie's voice: It's just the spirits, duffer, keep going.

For a time, I can't think what to do and then there's movement up ahead and it's a person not rags, I can see that now. They're rising and there's a crack in the sky and that's thunder and after there's a flash and that's lightning but it's the wrong order, and now there's sun, it's appeared out of nowhere. The figure is walking, they're coming towards the car. They're holding up one hand and it's a thumb, they've stuck their thumb out either wanting a ride, wanting to leave or rather saying everything is fine, here is okay, that they aren't dangerous. I can't tell if they're woman, if they're woman, man or other. Their head is covered by a hood and maybe they're good and maybe they're bad and why won't my feet work, why won't my brain skip to a clear answer. It's not about matchboxes and it's not about the dog in space or a red beret or the flavours of gum. It's not about the painting of hell either. It's about beauty and safety. I don't have my hurdy and I don't have a bell, there's no centre for me and no edges here. What I do have is the air that is around me with the earth at my feet and the sky up above. And I have certainty about one thing. I know that the world is wild and wide, it's the only thing I'm sure of. Wide and wild. It's both.

ACKNOWLEDGEMENTS

THANKS ARE DUE to my publisher Jane Palfreyman and all at Allen & Unwin. To my agent Grace Heifetz at Left Bank Literary for loving it hard and getting what I was trying to do as soon as she read it. To Pam Ackland and Janine Mikosza for reading as a work in progress.

Thank you to Creative Victoria for the 2016 VicArts Grant awarded to develop this project back when it was called something else. This allowed me a research trip to Sydney where I met and spoke with circus expert Mark St Leon who gave generously of his time and knowledge. I visited the Powerhouse Museum twice in 2016 and was given access to the circus archives (thank you Paul Wilson and Peter Cox at the Museum of Applied Arts and Sciences), and thank you to Karen and Dimity in the Powerhouse library for letting me spend a day taking notes.

Hurdy Gurdy was written with the support of two residencies. Thank you to Bundanon Trust and the focused time a 2017 fellowship visit afforded me to work on this project. Thank you also to the very special Stella Grasstrees Writing Retreat, supported by the Trawalla Foundation, where I spent three incredibly productive weeks in November 2019 just before the world changed.

All my novels involve research and for this one there were many texts over many years, but the following were especially important in the concept-building, development and writing of this book:

Clown, Jon Davison, Bloomsbury Publishing, 2013

'Laughter in the Dark: Humour under Stalin', Iain Lauchlan. Published in *Le rire européen/European Laughter*, Alastair Duncan (ed.), University of Stirling, 2010, pp. 257–274. (For the *anekdoty* that appear in the novel)

Hammer and Tickle: A History of Communism Told Through Communist Jokes, Ben Lewis, Orion, 2009

The Silver Road: The Life of Mervyn King, Circus Man, as told to Mark St Leon, Butterfly Books, 1990

Take a Drum and Beat It: The Story of the Astonishing Ashtons, 1848–1900s, Judy Cannon with Mark St Leon, Tytherleigh Press, 1997

'The Congress of Clowns and Other Russian Circus Acts', Joel Schechter. *The Slavic and East European Journal*, Vol. 43, No. 2, 1999, pp. 402–404

Ryll's Diary—artefact, written by Marizles Wirth in 1945, held at Powerhouse Museum library, original document

ADDITIONAL NOTES

The quotation 'clowning is not a red nose but a free head' is from the great Russian clown, Slava Polunin, given to one of my characters in the book.

The matchbox routine that appears in the novel is a skit from the show 'Exceptions to Gravity', which has been borrowed from *Clown*, by Jon Davison (and Davison's transcription from video).

'It Couldn't Please Me More (A Pineapple)'—a song from *Cabaret*, released 1966—has been 'adjusted' and included.